A WEST RANCH CHRISTMAS

KATHY FAWCETT

Cover by Steve Fawcett

❀ Created with Vellum

CHAPTER 1

"It's getting dark so early, isn't it?"

Daisy took a deep breath of the chilled mountain air. With her free hand, she turned the collar up on her shearling coat, then gave the horse a gentle nudge with her boot to catch up with her date. Rowdy West slowed his roan down so they were once again side by side.

It was the middle of November, and he had invited her to go for an evening ride, so they could choose and tag a Christmas tree for his log house. He would come back for it another day, he told her. Not that she would have minded helping him cut it down, but neither wanted to subject a horse to dragging it home when an ATV would make quick work of it.

"Maybe we should have left a little sooner. But it's not much further; the grove of trees I thought we'd try is right up there." Rowdy smiled and pointed ahead.

Daisy couldn't help but smile back at the tall handsome cowboy who had captured her heart several months before—she'd follow him anywhere. To a dark, forbidden forest, even.

They had been introduced by a mutual friend, Paislee West, who asked Daisy if she'd go to his house and discuss a few pieces of original artwork for Rowdy's new walls.

"The previous owners left a paint-by-numbers barn," Paislee said, "and a mirrored beer sign with Clydesdales."

Money was no object, Paislee implied. Though humble and unassuming, the Wests were the largest landowners in the county, and possibly Wyoming.

Rowdy was a family cousin from Montana, the last of the bunch from the northern state. After selling off his own ranch and retiring from his rodeo days, he helped run the family ranch in West Gorge, and lived a quiet life when not at work. Daisy was sure she'd seen him coming out of the Mercantile, and driving through West Gorge in his truck—alone.

After their first introduction, they set about finding the most captivating landscapes to grace his "bachelor cabin," as he called it. In reality, it was a massive log structure with soaring ceilings, a fieldstone fireplace, and a state-of-the-art kitchen with heavy brass and cast iron appliances and fixtures.

But all Daisy could see when he opened his door that first time was his warm smile and kind eyes. He grinned at her like a kid finding Santa Claus at the door on Christmas morning, knowing he'd been a very good boy. After months of dating, Rowdy still had that wonderstruck look when they sat across from each other at dinner, or stole a kiss in the art gallery she owned in town.

Daisy had just about given up on love when this incredible man came into her life. He adored her, she could tell, and all she had to do was be herself. Rowdy loved her cooking, and her parents, and her little house in the middle of town. He laughed at her corny jokes and pretended to be interested in art history and the Renaissance era.

He made her feel beautiful, even wearing a sweatshirt and cleaning the gallery. But his kind eyes had a special spark to them when she wore her more romantic lace blouses with faded blue jeans, and let her wavy hair fall long and loose on her shoulders.

She was in love with the man soon after they met. Head over heels, in fact. And while she sometimes felt impatient for Rowdy to share his heart, she was glad to discover more about him in the waiting.

Conscious of a slight limp from his rodeo days, Rowdy had a bruise on his heart to match, she soon learned, which made him cautious.

Rowdy West was a man of honor—he meant what he said, and chose his words carefully.

He protected her. He was kind to animals, children, and all the hands at West Ranch. Rowdy was soft-spoken, which made the salt and pepper stubble and chiseled jawline that much more attractive.

He was patient, and just as old-fashioned as she was—something that tested her resolve more than once, as Rowdy's affection became more tender and lovely with each goodnight kiss on her doorstep.

A shiver went up Daisy's spine as she caught his reflection in the setting sun. She hardly noticed that he'd jumped off the horse and had taken the reigns from her.

"Let me help you down, Daisy," he said, looking up and catching her eyes.

Another shiver—and not from the cold.

Rowdy reached up and took hold of her waist, then slowly lowered her. He was so strong and steady, and very close to her as her feet touched the forest floor. Before she knew it, she was standing in his arms, tipping her face up for a soft kiss. They laughed a little as snowflakes fell on their faces, tickling their skin.

"I don't know how we're going to find a Christmas tree with the light so dim, sweetheart," she whispered.

He kissed her again. Maybe he'd forgotten about the tree.

"Hey," he said, taking a step back from her, "stay here. Let me see if I can shine some light on the situation."

As Rowdy walked deeper into the circle of pines, Daisy turned to look over her shoulder at the mountains and gorge. Snow capped the tall peaks, and settled on top of the rocks and trees near the river, giving it a storybook glow. She had long admired the painters and artists who had tried to capture the beauty of Wyoming, but nobody could touch the magnificence of the real deal.

Out of the corner of her eye, Daisy sensed light—a lot of light—and wondered if Rowdy brought a lantern. When she turned her head to look, nothing prepared her for the sight that awaited her.

CHAPTER 2

Daisy gasped, and brought her hands up to her face in shock. The tall trees encircling them were lit with thousands of twinkling lights. And in the center of it all, a hay bale stood surrounded by candlelit lanterns, and covered with a wool throw.

Do you see this? Daisy wanted to ask Rowdy, but of course he did—he orchestrated it.

Rowdy walked over and gently took Daisy's hand, and led her to the middle of the fairy tale forest of twinkling, flickering lights.

"Will you sit down, please?" As he spoke, she thought she detected a slight quiver of nervousness in his voice.

Daisy sat down, but not before a wave of adrenaline shot through her own body. Butterflies, feeling like they were made of steel, fluttered around in her stomach like raging tigers. She caught Rowdy's eye to try and make sense of everything, but when she did, the words were not there.

She remained silent as he knelt down in front of her, his blue jeaned leg resting in the snow.

Oh Rowdy, darling, she wanted to exclaim, *that can't be good for you...*

"Daisy."

"Yes, Rowdy?"

"Will you please," he pleaded with his eyes and voice, "do me the great honor of becoming my wife?"

She didn't want to take her eyes off of his own eyes, or his beautiful mouth, which had kissed her hundreds of times. But he drew her gaze to the tiny box he was opening. A bright, shining ring, set with a large emerald cut diamond sat in a bed of velvet.

"It's breathtaking," she said through tears.

"You're breathtaking," he said.

His poor leg. Daisy knew he'd asked her a monumental question, but all she could think about was how sore his leg would be from being in the snow. She knew he wouldn't get up until she answered.

"Yes… yes, I'll marry you," she managed at last, through choked tears. "Of course. There's no one but you."

As they stood, she could see small tears in his eyes too, which touched her heart.

"Here then," he whispered gruffly through his emotion, "let's see if this fits."

She held out her shaking hand as he caught her eyes. Then, taking her fingers in his larger, rougher, very capable cowboy hands, he slowly slipped the ring on her. She thought it would be cold, but it was warm and smooth.

Gasping, she held her hand up.

"Do you like it?" He was shy as he asked.

Do I like it?

She wanted to laugh, but wouldn't risk hurting his feelings. That was like asking if she liked the Wind River Mountains, or a Wyoming sunset; did she like chocolate; did she like being in love for the first time in her life when she'd nearly given up hope.

"Very much," she said instead. I like it and I love *you,* and can't wait to be your wife."

She fell into his arms and let him twirl her around as the forest lights bounced off the reflection of the cut jewels. Then, a gust of wind blew and he drew her close to his beating heart. She gladly nestled inside his arms, never taking her eyes off the stunning engagement ring on her hand as it rested on his shoulder.

. . .

"How about this Saturday, at the courthouse?" He was serious, she knew, as they sat in his house together, warming up in front of the stone fireplace. "We can wake up together Sunday morning."

"Tempting," Daisy answered with a smile. "How about… Christmas Eve, instead?"

"That's six long weeks away!"

He was protesting, but the smile on his face told her how happy he was to have a date when they would be married.

"Six short weeks, I say," she said, caressing his face, "planning even a small wedding takes a little time, sweetheart."

The fullness of the grin on his face was new to her—he was truly happy. And it almost made her want to go with him to the courthouse that very minute, and be his wife by midnight. He brought his smile down to her own lips and kissed her, and as she felt his mouth trembling against her own, six weeks suddenly felt very far away.

But it would fly by, wouldn't it?

"Christmas Eve it is," he said, when he took a breath. "But not a minute later."

"Agreed, cowboy," she whispered. "Mrs. West by Christmas."

CHAPTER 3

The West Ranch office building rattled, buffeted by early winds. The massive furnace was blowing away, doing all it could to warm the raftered ceiling and cement floors.

Inside, laughter and booming voices drowned each other out, as seven large men stood around a picnic table raising glasses of soda. There was Ridge West, the patriarch of the bunch, and his sons, Gunnar, Pike, Colton and Ash. Cousins Rowdy and Gray completed the family circle.

"Here's to a Christmas wedding," Gunnar said to the group, "and to the new Mrs. West. May she know what she's getting into."

"Here here," Colton said, as the others laughed. "Congratulations on finally getting the courage up, you ol' coward."

All eyes turned to Rowdy, who was blushing with delight.

"I would be an idiot to let Daisy get away," he said. "I have Paislee to thank for introducing us, the way she did." Rowdy nodded at Pike, Paislee's husband, who looked pleased at the compliment.

The women had been long-time friends and fellow lovers of art. It was Paislee who sent Daisy to Rowdy's place in West Gorge to help him put the finishing touches on his new log home. It wasn't long before sparks were flying, and not just in the fieldstone fireplace.

"My wife knows a masterpiece when she sees one," Pike said with a smile. "She's delighted to have Daisy joining the family—and, at their favorite spot in town, the West Gorge Arts and Culture Center. It's going to be the social event of the year."

"That's not saying much."

Always one for a joke, Colton West laughed and pointed out the other so-called social events held at the Culture Center. "There was the Wyoming taxidermy banquet, a high school class reunion, and a retirement party for Bud Shire and his wife last month."

"True, true," Pike said, defending his wife's efforts to make the community aware of the newest venue in town, "but Rowdy and Daisy's wedding will show it off in its best light. Maybe we'll even get a few new photos for the website."

"Hmmm," Rowdy grumbled. He wasn't thrilled at being the center of a social event of any kind, let alone having his picture show up on any website as the model groom. Not anymore; not since a zealous bucking bronco abruptly ended his successful rodeo days, leaving him with a prominent limp and a deeply embedded scowl.

The courthouse wedding was looking better and better to him, but Daisy, he knew, was enjoying the whirlwind of attention and activity surrounding the planning of their wedding. He would give that girl just about anything within his power—the woman who had looked past his limp and rough exterior, to discover the pain and longing underneath.

He was a die-hard romantic, too, which these cowboys could never know. Secretly, the thought of seeing Daisy in a frilly lace wedding dress, and an even frillier gown on their wedding night, made his already sore leg just about give out from under him.

"How many shopping days until Christmas?" Rowdy asked the circle, triggering another wave of good-natured laughter and hearty claps on the back.

CHAPTER 4

"Goodness, the Wests don't believe in long engagements, do they?" Sassy Tate was standing in the kitchen of the ranch house, helping to clean up after a big family dinner. They gathered to celebrate the engagement and strategize about the big day.

"I don't know, six weeks seems decadent," Kat said, hand-drying crystal goblets with a linen towel. "Gunnar and I were married in a West Ranch meadow, just a few weeks after he proposed. Paislee, how long was it before you and Pike got married?"

Paislee smiled while putting leftover food in storage containers.

"Hmm, let's see," she said. "Pike showed up in Denver with an engagement ring and the wedding took place… about ten days later. Just so happened, my mama had several dates on hold with the country club. Only… she had a different groom in mind. Until she met Pike West that is, and couldn't picture me with anyone but him. Liu, what about you and Colton?"

Liu Chen West sat at the kitchen table with her hands on her growing belly. She rubbed around and around as the others brought her cups of tea and mild biscuits to ease her discomfort and indigestion.

It wasn't like the girl to sit and rest.

"Colton built me the teahouse and then proposed at the end of my first summer on the ranch," she said, "we were married a few weeks later, just as the aspen trees were turning yellow."

"Sheesh," Sassy exclaimed in surprise. "The Wests do move fast."

All the women in the room laughed, while Kat nudged her playfully with her elbow. "Yes, they do," Kat said. "Be forewarned, little sister."

Sassy smiled, and dipped her head to hide the embarrassment.

"Ridge and I were married in just days," Casey volunteered. "I guess when you have friends at the courthouse, you can pull a string or two."

"He just couldn't wait," Kat said with a smile.

"Neither could I," Casey blushed.

"I guess six weeks seems like an eternity in light of everyone else," Daisy said, "but a week has gone by already since Rowdy proposed, and next week is Thanksgiving. Then the wedding is just a month away."

The others could hear a slight panic in her voice.

"Is it the last Thanksgiving in your parents' house, Daisy?" The Shires had recently retired, and Bud Shire sold his drugstore and pharmacy practice to a big chain store that was building a new location on the edge of town. The Shires would be moving to a warmer climate.

"Yep," Daisy said. "It will be our last holiday season together in West Gorge. They'll be leaving the day after the wedding—on Christmas. The house sold last week."

"Wow, that was fast," Liu chimed in from the background.

"It *was* fast," said real estate agent Casey, "and don't mention it in front of Ridge. He came home in a snit when he found out. He always thought Bud would sell that house to him when it was time."

Daisy looked sheepish at the conversation.

"Oh I'm sorry, Daisy," Casey said, "I wasn't thinking. Of course your parents have a right to sell to whoever they want to. It's just a beautifully built home, so lovingly cared for through the years. That kind of vintage quality is hard to replicate."

"Unless it's replicated by master builder, Colton West," Liu said with a smile.

"He's so much in demand, Liu, people better be prepared to wait a while," Paislee said, to general nods and consent. "Everyone wants a home by Colton—my friends are always asking me to pull some strings."

"Hey, I was surprised about mom and dad selling, too," Daisy said. "I always dreamed I'd own that house myself, someday. But I guess that's not practical, now that Rowdy has made the log house his home."

"Right, the in-town bungalow couldn't compete with the corrals and barns you and Rowdy will have," Kat said.

"Just think, Daisy," Paislee said, "all those blank walls, crying out for paintings."

After more good-natured laughter, all the women settled in around the big ranch table with cups of coffee and a platter of cookies.

"Now then," Kat said, presiding over the council of West women, "what's everyone doing for Thanksgiving? And more importantly, what are we all wearing to Daisy's Christmas Eve wedding?"

CHAPTER 5

Two hours later, the women were winding down and yawning around the table. Sassy excused herself and slipped out of the kitchen, then walked quietly into the darkened great room. The only light came from a few lit candles and the fireplace, which had tamped down into embers and small flames.

Once her eyes adjusted, Sassy could see the room was empty. Gunnar had carried a sleeping Willow to her bed, and Pike and Colton were talking quietly in a nearby den, where Sun and Ford slept on a sofa. Ridge, Rowdy, and Gray sat outside on a lower level porch, huddled around an outdoor firepit. Some of the women were gathering their warmest wraps and furs to go join them.

She didn't see Ash among any of the groups and wondered if he'd slipped off to bed. Sassy herself had been invited by Kat to stay the night in one of the guestrooms, which she gladly agreed to.

"That way you can stay and enjoy the family for as long as you'd like," Kat said. "After the kids fall asleep, many of us catch a second wind and stay up pretty late playing cards, or just talking about life."

Kat had become a true big sister to Sassy, beyond her wildest hopes. She made time to meet for lunch during the week, and even planned shopping trips together. Gray West had been roped in by the

West women to fly them to Denver for a few days for early Christmas shopping. They would all stay at the Andrews mansion, and shop 'til they dropped.

"You might need to fly back for all our packages, Gray," Kat had teased.

Sassy felt at home at the big house when she was there, whether she was with Ash or not. But they had been dating steadily since her return to West Gorge, so she felt a little miffed that he didn't at least say goodnight to her—they were, after all, under the same roof. Maybe she should send him a text…

"Hey, beautiful." Sassy felt two strong arms wrap around her from behind just then, while a low, sexy voice spoke warmly into her curls.

Ash West.

"Mmm," she murmured with deep satisfaction, allowing him to nuzzle her neck and shoulders. "I was just getting a little angry with you, thinking you'd gone off to bed."

"Without you?... I mean, without telling you?"

"Stop with the teasing, Ash," she scolded gently.

They had an agreement that their relationship would not go beyond kissing, but some days that took a lot of resolve. Some nights, it took an outright miracle. Especially on nights like this, when he was gently pulling her by the hand to curl up on the floor in front of a fire. Or when his eyes looked at her the way they did in the warm light. It would have been easy to slip unnoticed into her room or his.

"So, what were all you ladies discussing in the kitchen?"

"What do you think?" Sassy answered. "Daisy and Rowdy's Christmas Eve wedding."

Ash smiled. "I'm happy for Rowdy; for them both."

"Me too," Sassy said, stretching her feet out as they leaned back on plush pillows propped against the log and steel coffee table.

"A Christmas wedding must be every little girl's dream."

"A lot of little girls would answer in the affirmative," Sassy laughed softly.

"What about *this* little girl?" Ash had his arm around Sassy, and tapped her on the shoulder.

Sassy shifted her body sideways so she could see Ash's face as they talked. She was struck with how much he'd matured since their first attempts at dating, back in the summer. Then, he was all arms and elbows, and more than a little anxious about so many things. Now, he was more serious, but still loving and thoughtful; and yes, playful. She was glad about that.

He was also more eager to find out about her dreams and plans than worried that their two worlds might not align.

Ash removed the pressure for her to stay in Wyoming, which allowed Sassy's love for the mountains and gorge to grow on its own. Or maybe *she* was growing in her love for Ash, making the beauty of Wyoming that much sweeter.

"Funny, I don't think I have a dream wedding," she said with all honesty. "I never pictured a big affair—I guess I picture the marriage itself as my dream. And after losing my dad the way I did, and everything else, my dream marriage is one where the husband doesn't have a previous, secret family."

"Seems a reasonable expectation," he said softly. Ash knew that the "everything else" Sassy referred to was the painful realization that her father had abandoned his first wife and child to pursue another woman—Sassy's mother.

Ash lifted his hand and sweetly cupped the side of her face as she spoke. His eyes reflected the pain she felt, and she loved him all the more for it.

"Besides," Sassy continued, "I honestly don't think I could have an actual wedding where I invite both my sister and my mother. I wouldn't want to make Kat or Sugar uncomfortable by being at the same event, and I couldn't leave either out of such a big day."

"But..." Ash seemed distressed. "That's not fair to you."

"It's okay," she said, "we both know life isn't fair, Ash. But we do know that life can be very, very good."

Sassy leaned over and punctuated her words with feathery brushes on Ash's lips.

"Yes, *very* good," he mumbled through kisses.

CHAPTER 6

"You're up late, Liu," Paislee leaned over and said, while tucking a wool throw around her very pregnant sister-in-law. The two were outside, sitting around an outdoor fireplace. All the children were asleep, and the adults were enjoying a late Autumn evening. Soon, they all knew, the snow would force them indoors for a long winter, and they wanted to soak up every outdoor chance they could get.

"Who can sleep with this huge baby, kicking and pushing me around," Liu said. Her voice sounded disgruntled, but her eyes and smile betrayed her excitement and joy.

"Three more weeks," Paislee said. "It will fly by—unless you go late."

"Chens are never late," Liu said.

Just then, Colton came outside bearing a mug of cocoa for his wife, and warm wool slippers. Gently, he lifted each of Liu's feet and slid the slippers on, then handed her the hot chocolate. As he kissed the top of her head, he reminded her that the baby would be half West.

"Ah, but the Wests are always on time, too," Liu said. "This baby is doomed to a punctual life; a life filled with Chinese spring rolls, BBQ sliders, and an identity crisis. Should he be a cowboy, or an engineer?"

The group outside laughed quietly at Liu's observation.

"Or she might be a chef. Or the next visionary builder of a bigger, better West Gorge, Wyoming," Colton volunteered as he reached over for Liu's hand.

The two of them knew the lengths they had gone to just to have the careers they loved, in spite of their family's reservations. They both wished to create an easier future for their firstborn.

"Let's just get this baby safely into the world, before we ask him or her to pick their university and job path." Kat tried to sound light-hearted, but as a physician, and a Wyoming rancher, she knew that the baby's due date was like a speeding train heading to town—and so was winter weather. "Liu, Colton, my offer still stands for you two to stay at my condo until you deliver. You could practically walk to the hospital from there. I'd feel so much better about this little one's December arrival."

"Thank you, Kat," Liu sounded sincere. "But my mother and grandmother practically live with us, and they can help."

"Liu," Kat challenged, "I can't even guess how old your grandmother is. You know I love her, but her vision is not what it used to be. And your mother is an accountant, not a midwife."

Without saying so, Kat resolved to beef up her medical supplies that she kept at the ranch and in the house—just in case; to be prepared for more than just a scrape or cut.

"Maybe we should really think about it, Liu," Colton said, concern shadowing his face.

"Historically speaking," Gunnar spoke up and everyone turned towards him, "the West family hasn't fared well with early season blizzards. We almost lost Dad and Casey in that blizzard a few years ago. If the wolves didn't get them, the cold would have."

Ridge reached over and took Casey's hand.

"Yes, the blizzards are no joke," Paislee concurred. "I was half frozen on the doorstep of the old homestead when Pike found me."

"But *girl*, he so warmed you up," Daisy said, to general laughter and a few hoots.

In the dark, nobody could see Paislee blush as she laughed, but Pike's broad grin was visible in the firelight.

"Maybe, just this once, the snow will hold off," Rowdy said, hopefully. "We can safely welcome Colton and Liu's baby in December, and have a Christmas Eve wedding without incident."

"Every girl's dream," Daisy deadpanned to laughter, "a wedding without *incident*."

CHAPTER 7

"We should have told them, Pike," Paislee spoke quietly as they carried Sun and Ford into their house in West Gorge Woods later that night. Since moving in, they'd filled the walls with colorful abstracts and watercolors, and original oil paintings by none other than Pike West. On the floor, equally colorful toys were strewn about, but thankfully, they left a clear path to the stairway before heading to the ranch.

Since getting married, Pike and Paislee enjoyed their close proximity to the West family home for nights such as these. Pike could have dinner with his dad and brothers, without feeling the need to talk "shop" about the workings of the ranch. He treasured the time he spent painting his landscapes, and was constantly amazed by his wife's support.

"I know, everybody was there," Pike agreed, "but there never seemed to be the right opening—and the night was really more about the wedding, and Rowdy and Daisy."

"I get it. But we have to share our news sooner or later."

"Thanksgiving, I guess."

"Deal," Paislee said. "I do hope these little ones sleep in tomorrow, so we can too."

"Fat chance," Pike laughed softly. "But sleep is overrated, I think."

Paislee looked at her husband, never more handsome than when he was tucking in their children and kissing them on the tops of their heads. That he clearly loved and adored little adopted Sun just as much as their flesh-and-blood boy, made her heart beat wildly for the man. As he straightened his lanky frame and turned to her, she could see delight and surprise register on his face as she caught his gaze and reached for his hand.

"Sleep is overrated, huh?" Paislee moved her arms up to wrap around his shoulders. "Tell me more."

"We should have told everyone tonight, don't you think, Ridge?"

Casey looked back at Ridge, who quietly closed the door to their bedroom suite at the ranch. They had stayed up late, talking and laughing with the family after a celebratory dinner in honor of Rowdy and Daisy.

"Mmm," Ridge answered, noncommittally, "maybe."

"When will everyone be together again the way we were tonight?"

"Thanksgiving, the wedding, and Christmas," Ridge answered.

"But then it will be too late," Casey argued.

"Right, we may need to spread the word one by one," he said. "But more importantly, did you find out from Daisy who bought Bud Shire's house? I can't believe someone beat me to the draw on that Craftsman bungalow. I've had my eye on it for years."

"I know you have," Casey commiserated. "Daisy didn't seem to know anything."

"That son of a gun, Bud," Ridge grumbled. "I thought he was a friend. Now I have to be nice to him at the wedding, when what I want to do is throttle him."

"He is a friend, Ridge," Casey cautioned, "one of your oldest friends. I'm sure he didn't think you still wanted it after all this time—you do own so much, you know. We have a beautiful house in

Phoenix, too. Completely remodeled from head to toe. To our specifications and tastes."

"I know," Ridge pouted. "There's no logical reason for me to buy Bud's house."

"No, there isn't. You sound a bit… spoiled," Casey said, though not unkindly.

Ridge smirked at the suggestion, then focused on his wife.

"I'm not really spoiled," he drawled. "I just appreciate that house. It's a fine piece of craftsmanship, like I've rarely seen. You know I'm a sucker for… craftsmanship."

As he held Casey's gaze, he reached up and caressed her tanned arm. She had just pulled her dress over her head, and stood before him with pajamas in hand.

"The level of perfection and the fine lines…" he said with a crooked grin as he moved closer to her.

Casey's mouth dropped open with delight, as Ridge drew her to him.

"Hmm. Are we still talking about…" she whispered.

"No. No, we aren't," he whispered back, before leaning in to kiss her.

CHAPTER 8

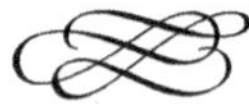

"No secrets, Sheriff," Gunnar said as he crawled into bed next to Kat. She was half asleep, but held just the hint of an uncharacteristic scowl on her face. "What's eating you?"

"I don't know what you mean…" she tried, to no avail.

"Yes, you do," he said quietly. "Something's bothering you about this wedding."

Kat exhaled fully and rolled towards Gunnar.

"I love Daisy. I love everything about her marrying Rowdy, except one thing. Her twin sister, Darlene."

Darlene Shire was Gunnar's girlfriend years before. Gunnar had asked her to consider marrying him and she declined, then moved away. Eventually she realized how foolish that had been, but by then Kat and Gunnar had fallen hard for each other during the most romantic quarantine ever.

"Like a bad penny, she's going to show up and ruin the big day for me, and all the special events ahead—births, baptisms… you name it. She'll be there."

"I'm sorry, Kat, I truly am. If it's any consolation, I haven't given her a thought since the day we met. I barely gave her a thought when we were dating. And honestly, if she's just as selfish as I remember, she won't be at any of Daisy's special events."

"She'll be at the wedding, for sure."

"Probably, but only because her parents are moving and she'll want to see them; maybe get some money from them. See what valuable items in their house she can sell."

"Wow, such a catch. To think, she could have been the mother of your children."

"All I can say is that the good Lord protected me from my own foolishness," Gunnar spoke softly in the dark. "If He hadn't, Darlene would have turned this beautiful ranch into a glorified *She Shed,* bled the West Foundation dry to the bone for her own selfish purposes, and sent me running to the hills with regret, to live like a wild homeless hermit."

Kat couldn't help but laugh at the imagery.

"Stop," she implored Gunnar.

"No, I mean it, Kat," he said with sincerity in his voice. "You are a great treasure to me, and to this family. I know I don't deserve you, but I thank God every day that you love me. You breathed life into this dry, dusty, grieving family, and look at us now—we have an overflowing home, filled with love and color and laughter... you created a place we all want to be, every one of us."

Kat felt a lump in her throat at Gunnar's words, and felt tears trickle down her face and into her pillow. A man of few words, when her husband did speak from his heart, it was something to drink in.

"Kat West," Gunnar went on, "you resurrected my mother's foundation which blesses this entire community. You whipped that hospital into shape. You are the most amazing mother to our daughter. And you make my heart go pitty-pat every day."

By this time, Kat had worked her way into the crook of Gunnar's arm, which eagerly held her tight.

"As far as the Christmas Eve wedding goes," he said into her lush silky hair, "every other woman ought to be nervous about seeing *you* —because you are Doctor Kat *flipping* West, and don't you forget it. I never do."

CHAPTER 9

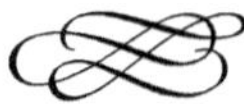

"I'd take *you* home, if I could, cowboy," the woman crooned as Ash squirmed uncomfortably. Slightly round in the middle and wrapped in a wool shawl, she was standing in the Amber Waves store, ready to show Ash West where to put her packages.

"Just show me your car, ma'am, please..." Ash said, walking out the door. It wasn't his first leer of the day, but it was the first outright proposition.

Coming back in the store, he caught the eye of both Amber and Sassy, and they all laughed.

"I thought gorging on turkey and stuffing on Thanksgiving was supposed to make you sleepy—but these ladies are downright frisky," Ash said. "I need a coffee break."

"Take all the time you need, as long as it's ten minutes," Amber said. "I'm so grateful for the extra help for my Black Friday sale. I had no idea the turnout would be so big."

"I'm glad I wore comfortable shoes," Sassy said. "Amber, there seems to be a lull. Why don't you go sit and have coffee too, and I'll keep an eye on things."

"Thanks Sassy, no argument here," Amber said, falling into a chair by the coffee station. There, the aroma of French Roast filled the air, as the coffee stood hot and ready for customers. A platter of star-shaped cookies sat on a platter, sprinkled with red and green sugar. All around the store, lights twinkled and cranberry candles flickered.

Sassy walked to the front of the store where a group of women were filling their shopping baskets with "Merry ChrisMoose" mugs and dessert plates. Looking over her shoulder, she was happy to see Amber and Ash enjoying a much deserved rest, and laughing together like the old friends they were.

Sometimes Sassy wondered if the two would fall in love for real if she was out of the picture for good, but wasn't about to find out. Ash West 2.0 was all she could ever want in a first true love. There were a few weeks between the time she left him after their heated blow-up, and the time he discovered she'd returned to West Gorge, but it was long enough to right their ship. With Sassy promising to stay until Christmas, and no hidden secrets between them, they were able to relax and be the best versions of themselves possible.

Thinking back to the family dinner at the ranch house, it felt so right to kiss Ash by the fireplace of the family home, with the stars in the sky visible from the massive windows. The memories of him coming up behind her and slipping his arms around her, whispering in her ear, still caused Sassy's legs to tingle.

Now, with Christmas just four weeks away, Ash still didn't seem anxious. He wasn't pressuring her for answers, but she was beginning to pressure herself. Was she going to stay? Could she really walk away from Ash's touch… from his kisses and his caring?

"I just don't know!" Sassy said out loud, causing one shopper to misunderstand, and exclaim, *"could you find out then... If Amber is going to restock those adorable bayberry candles, that is?"*

"Oh… oh sure," Sassy said, recovering and walking towards Amber. As she did, Wayne, the summer ranch hand and nephew of West family friends, Jackie and Red, walked in. Red owned the town's BBQ restaurant, and was now selling his bottled sauce nationwide. Wayne looked older than Sassy remembered, and taller. He went straight to Amber and planted a proprietary kiss on her lips, then set a large box by the coffee station.

"Red sends his regards, and BBQ sliders with slaw," he told the threesome. "Now, what can I do to help?"

"Oh Wayne," Amber gushed, "you're my hero."

"Oh *Wayne*," Ash mocked, taking off his Amber Waves apron and tossing it to Wayne, "you're my hero, *toooo*."

While chewing on a big bite of a sandwich, Sassy said, "I'd laugh if I weren't so tired and hungry. Who knew that running a little Christmas store could be more exhausting than roping a steer, or hauling dead trees out of a muddy creek?"

Neither Amber or Wayne paid any attention to the conversation around them. As Amber ate the last bites of a slider, Wayne slipped the apron over his head and tied it around his waist. Just then, the Christmas music playing through the store speakers changed to Bing Crosby crooning "I'm dreaming of a white Christmas, just like the ones I used to know…"

"May I have this dance?" Wayne held his hand out to Amber with a smile.

"But… my store," she protested weakly.

"It's called *work life balance*," Wayne said smoothly, not taking no for an answer.

As Sassy and Ash watched, Amber put her arm around Wayne's shoulder and the two swayed back and forth in a clearing by the cash register. The handful of customers, all women, stopped their shopping and watched the two, transfixed.

"Awww, would you look at that," one of them said, wiping a tear from her eye.

"My Fred used to dance with me in the kitchen," another lamented.

"Is this a bad time to ask Amber about the candles, do you think?" Said a third.

CHAPTER 10

"The caterers want to know what to serve at our wedding besides a beef dish," Daisy said to Rowdy over dinner.

The two were dining by candlelight at a lakeside chalet outside of town. In the corner of the chalet stood a tall Frasier fir decorated with twinkling white lights and red ornaments. Poinsettias lined the hearth of the stone fireplace, which was crackling and glowing to warm the cold night.

"The only thing better than a beef dish," Rowdy said, "is *two* beef dishes."

"Traditionally, there's chicken or fish," Daisy offered, "or a pasta dish, for vegans."

"I thought we agreed not to invite vegans to our wedding," Rowdy said. "I certainly don't know any, do you?"

"Maybe my kooky sister, I never know with her. And, full disclosure, I have my vegan days," Daisy answered with a smile. "But I'll put you down for... what, beef maybe?"

"Honestly, I think I'll be too nervous to eat," Rowdy said, putting his fork down and looking straight at Daisy.

"You're joking! My big strong cowboy—nervous?"

Rowdy dipped his head slightly and Daisy could see that he wasn't joking at all. She felt alarmed to think she hadn't realized something so important about her fiancée.

"I tend to avoid being the center of attention, Daisy, but I'll do it for you."

"Gosh, I'm sorry Rowdy. I never dreamed… but you were in the rodeo circuit for years, in front of hundreds and thousands of people. You don't get to that level without being a crowd pleaser."

"You're right. I used to be okay in crowds, but that was before," he said.

She wanted to ask *before what,* but as he rubbed his leg, she understood. Rowdy West was a big strong cowboy, but in social situations, he was bashful because of his injury.

Why hadn't she paid closer attention?

Daisy kicked herself. There was nothing she wanted more than to love him and care for him, in the tenderest way possible. If that meant putting his jangled nerves in front of her desire to walk down an aisle in a white gown, then so be it.

"I feel like an idiot, Rowdy," she said quietly, "assuming you and I were on the same page with this wedding. I apologize."

"Oh now wait a minute," he smiled broadly, "this has gone off the rails. We *are* on the same page with our wedding—I wouldn't want anything other than the beautiful wedding we're planning. I'm counting the days until you walk towards me and take my name."

"Really?" Daisy asked, placing her hand on his.

"Really," Rowdy answered. "All I said was that I might be too nervous to eat."

They looked at each other across the candlelight and laughed softly together.

"In that case, I'd better pay a pre-nuptial visit to the log house and stock the refrigerator before our wedding," Daisy smiled. "What's your favorite treat?"

Rowdy raised his eyebrows and leaned in conspiratorially, while crooking his finger.

"Come a little closer and I'll tell you."

Daisy laughed in surprise, and tingled as she leaned in to hear what he had to say. Instead, he closed the gap and brought his lips softly to hers.

"You. You are my favorite treat," he whispered.

CHAPTER 11

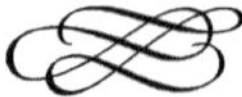

"Don't fall off that ladder, Pike."

Paislee stood in the great room of the West Ranch house, watching as her husband stretched his arm up and out to place a hammered tin star on the tall tree. Christmas music was playing in the background and the three children, Willow, Sun and Ford, were handily decorating the lower branches of the freshly-cut pine.

"While I'm up here, hand me some ornaments and I'll place them near the top," Pike said. "The tree is looking a bit *bottom-heavy,* thanks to the kids."

"Reminds me of a great aunt we once had," Gunnar joked as he stood back to take it in.

"Gunnar!" Kat's laugh had a gentle scold in it, but she went to where he stood and wrapped her arms around his waist. Gunnar held her tight and kissed the top of her head.

Colton and Liu weren't able make it for the tree trimming party; Liu was feeling slightly under the weather, and the two decided to stay close to home. Ash was helping Rowdy with some unexpected chores on the ranch, and Sassy couldn't break away from Amber's store, she said. Casey also had to cancel—she had been trying to hand off some of her property management business in order to retire and spend more time traveling with Ridge.

As for Ridge, he told Kat to call him when the tree was finished, and he'd enjoy the finished product.

"Scrooge," she'd called him when he said that, but he only laughed.

"You know, I put in my time, Kat," Ridge argued. "I've assembled bikes at four o'clock in the morning. I've made late night runs into town on Christmas Eve to find stocking stuffers when a certain woman couldn't find where she hid the shopping bag. For many years, I let little hands pull me bleary-eyed to the tree, to show me what Santa brought. But now it's your turn—yours, Gunnar's, Pike and Paislee's, and soon, Colton and Liu's."

Kat couldn't help but smile at the image of Ridge as a young father, jumping through hoops to make his family happy at Christmas.

"All right, I'll give you a pass," she said, "this time."

"Oh, I'll rally," Ridge told her. "Just you wait. Forget father Christmas—I'll be *Grandpa* Christmas when it's time."

"You'd better be," Kat said.

The others were missed, but it didn't stop Kat from enjoying the moment. The children were so excited about every ornament they pulled from the big box, and she loved watching their brilliant little minds at work.

Let's put all the snowmen really close together, so they can visit.

I'm going to hang this hot cocoa ornament next to baby Jesus, in case he's thirsty.

I'll hang these stars as high as I can reach, like real stars in the sky.

"This is the tree where Santa is going to leave toys for us," Sun said, turning around.

"Is that so?" Kat sat down on the sofa to be eye level with Sun and the other children. "Santa brings Willow's toys here, but won't he bring your toys to your house, Sun? Like always?"

Ford joined Sun and they both shook their heads.

"Aunt Kat, Mama said Santa Clause is going to bring our toys here this year," Ford informed the room. "She wrote him a letter, so I know it's true."

"Well then it must be true," Kat said with a smile, hugging her niece and nephew. Then to all the kids she said, "there's milk in the kitchen, and a plate of sandwiches and carrot sticks. After lunch we can decorate cookies."

When the kids were out of earshot, Kat looked up at Paislee.

"Sorry to blindside you, Kat," Paislee said, sitting down next to Pike, who had climbed down from the ladder. "We're going to Denver right after Christmas this year, and I didn't want to have to put away our decorations. You know how it is, with all the toys and everything, it's one thing too many this year."

"I get it," Kat said. "We only have Willow, and sometimes feel as though we're living in a toy store. We'd love to have Santa bring the kids' toys here."

"It will save him a trip," Gunnar said with a wink to Pike and Paislee as he sat down.

Pike dropped his gaze uncomfortably, and gave Paislee's hand a squeeze.

"I'll... go check on the kids," Pike said, "and get the cookies out."

"I'll come with you," Paislee said hurriedly, getting up to follow Pike out of the room.

"Well that wasn't strange at all," Kat said in the silence that followed. The only sound in the room was a Christmas carol on the radio. "Pike and Paislee seemed nervous. And guilty. Did they seem nervous to you?"

"Yep, even I could see that."

"What should we do?"

Gunnar looked over at Kat and smiled, then pulled her close.

"We should make out on this sofa like teenagers, and let Pike and Paislee decorate cookies with the kids," he said, "that's what we should do."

Kat laughed, thinking he was joking. But he wasn't.

CHAPTER 12

"Okay, I finally understand what the Mercantile is all about."

Sassy stood in the store in downtown West Gorge, flipping through a rack of flannel shirts. Her shopping cart was nearly full with fur-lined snow boots, flannel-lined jeans, long underwear, three pair of gloves, a rag wool hat and a sweater or two. When she first came to town, she thought West Gorge was a bit lacking in high fashion. But now it was December, and the first few snowfalls had been no joke—high fashion was off the table.

"It's all about the Wyoming winters," Ash said

"We sell plenty in the summer, too," the store owner shouted in Ash's direction. She had been outfitting Ash since long before he was a West, and wasn't above a little eavesdropping as he talked with the pretty blonde.

"I know," Ash said to the owner with a grin on his face, "but in the summer, the Mercantile is all about wants. In the winter, it's about *needs*—I need to stay warm. I need to stay dry. I need to not freeze my…"

"Careful," the owner said with a laugh.

"…my *toes* off," Ash recovered.

"Well, I need to ring you up before closing, and that's in ten minutes," she said. "I have a hot date tonight with a bowl of venison stew and a new episode of *Survivor.*"

Back on the street a short time later, Sassy and Ash pulled the collars up on their coats to block the wind spewing blasts of wet snow in their faces. Sassy tugged the rag wool hat out of the shopping bag—price tag and all—and pulled it low over her cold ears.

With bags from the Mercantile under their arms, they half ran to Sassy's apartment, two blocks away, being careful not to slip and slide on the iced sidewalk.

"Ho Ho holy cow, it's cold out there," Ash said minutes later, taking off his coat and boots just inside Sassy's door.

Sassy had done the same, after dropping all of her purchases on the floor. She traded her boots for wool slippers, her coat for a cardigan sweater, and left the hat on her head for the time being.

"Classy," Ash said, giving the price tag a flip and pulling Sassy into his arms.

"Are you warming me up?" She asked, hugging him tight, "or am I warming you up?"

"I'd give you just about anything, Sassy," Ash said as he kissed her cheek, "except my body heat right about now. I don't have much to spare."

She giggled a little into his flannel shirt, then gently pulled away.

"I made chicken soup this morning," she said, "that should warm us both up."

"Thank you. That sounds wonderful."

After his offer of help was politely declined, Ash sat on the sofa and put a thick throw over his legs, while watching Sassy at the small kitchen island. The apartment had been renovated to become an open concept, with everything visible except the washroom, which was behind a heavy wood door. The windows were original to the building, however, and not airtight. Wind rattled the leaded glass and cold air seeped under the sash.

"This is a drafty old place, isn't it?" Ash shivered, though the furnace was working hard to pump warm air into the apartment.

"Yes, it is," Sassy laughed. "Hot in the summer, and cold in the winter. But lots of charm, and the price is right. Good location, too. I can walk to the accounting job, and I love working with Amber in her store. Besides, everyone is supposed to have horror stories of their first apartment. Something to look back and laugh about when you're old and gray."

"Oh, I didn't realize you were going to turn old and gray... this could change things."

Sassy laughed and tossed a cloth napkin at him before bringing out a tray with two crocks of steaming soup, a basket of rolls, and two mugs of hot cocoa.

"Somehow I think you'll get there before I do," she said with a smile, reaching up to gently touch Ash on the side of his face. "I see a fleck of silver in your hair every now and then, in the right light."

Ash also reached up. He took her hand in his and brought it to his lips, then brushed her knuckles lightly.

"I'm sure you'll never be old *or* gray, Sassy," Ash said. "You'll just get smarter, and stronger and more beautiful with age."

"How do you know?" Sassy asked, perplexed at his confidence.

"I just do," he said.

And I want to be there to see it, he thought as his heart began to race.

Picking up their crocks of soup by the handles, Ash and Sassy brought them together for a light "clink," then settled into the sofa for a hot dinner.

"Tell me Ash, are you going to live at the ranch all winter? I can certainly understand the appeal in this weather. It's a short commute."

Ash shrugged. "I guess so. My renter left the bungalow in town so I could go back there if I want, or rent it out to skiers for the winter. Why do you ask—do you want to be my next door neighbor again?" He gave her a gentle nudge as he asked this.

"No, but you seem so... far away at the ranch," Sassy said carefully. "I'm not going to lie; I miss being close to you. I wonder how much I'll see you this month, now that I know what the weather is like here."

"Oh, this is nothing." Ash gestured to the window and the wind dismissively.

"Like I said, it's only going to get worse."

Sassy looked sad, suddenly, and Ash bit his lip to not ask the forbidden, unspoken question. *When are you leaving again, Sassy—are these our last few weeks together?*

He promised not to push her for a promise she couldn't make, but it felt like his heart was sitting at a red light, waiting for it to turn green. And he was chomping at the bit to go full steam ahead. Taking a deep breath, he asked the question in a roundabout way, and hoped for a Hail Mary pass.

"So, are you and your mother spending the holidays together?"

Sassy smiled and regarded his question.

"Funny you should ask, Ash. She called today and told me that she booked herself on a Christmas jazz cruise, with a singles group in her area. They sail on Christmas Eve, and return in the new year."

Ash couldn't contain his relief, and his raggedy sigh revealed all the tension he'd been holding in. Sassy reached over and put her hand on his, and it was warm from the soup bowl.

"I want you to know how much I appreciate you not pressuring me, Ash. I've really enjoyed dating these past few months, and you've been really great."

Sassy set her bowl on the coffee table and curled her feet up on the sofa. She burrowed into Ash as he wrapped his arm around her and pulled her close.

"That's me," Ash said quietly as he let his head fall back. "A really great guy."

CHAPTER 13

"Three weeks until Christmas, and two weeks until the baby is due," Kat told Liu. "I wish with all my heart that you and Colton would move into my condo while you wait. Colton will be nearby at the West Gorge Woods building site, and you'll be close to your doctor, and the hospital."

"I know, I know," Liu protested. "Still deliberating."

The women were in Liu's kitchen, where Ling and Chun were filling Chinese dumplings and simmering a chicken for stew. Without asking, Ling set a cup of tea in front of Kat and a plate of spring rolls and finger sandwiches.

"Chun thinks you need to eat," Liu's mother said with a sly smile. Chun turned around and nodded to Kat in silent agreement.

After a slight bow to both women, Kat reached out and hugged Ling, who welcomed the affection.

"Thank you, *Xièxiè nǐ*," she said to Chun and Ling. "I am rather hungry."

It was such a delight to have so many women in the extended family now, following the early lonely years on the ranch. First Paislee came, and then Liu, who began as the ranch chef and Kat's first hire.

Liu brought her entire family with her when she married Colton, multiplying their family in a wonderful way.

Kat turned back to Liu and her face reflected her concern. With a nod towards the window, she motioned towards the falling snow outside.

"Liu, your baby is quite large for someone as small as you. I'm sure your doctor is all over it, but you might very well deliver early, and the roads will be slow."

"Chen's are never early," Ling offered from the range, where she stirred the stew.

"Never late, and never early," Kat said with a laugh.

"Always right on... time," Liu said with a pained smile. Obviously, the baby was kicking and making Liu uncomfortable. Kat remembered how cumbersome she felt in the last month before Willow arrived, when the baby put pressure on her lungs, her bladder, her heart and her ribs. She peed every time she sneezed, and then cried to Gunnar as she tossed and turned at night about the alien that had taken over her body.

But of course, Willow was nothing but joy to her. Liu would quickly forget the discomfort, Kat knew—she just wanted to get her safely past the delivery. As Kat sipped her tea, Liu excused herself to go lay down. Chun followed to help provide any comforts she needed, and Kat was a little envious of this. Maybe her mother would have been as attentive, if she'd given her the chance.

Ling poured her own tea and sat next to Kat in the kitchen.

"Can you convince her, Ling?" Kat asked.

Ling shrugged and looked out the window with a faraway smile. "Liu stopped listening to me many years ago. Otherwise, she would have been a lawyer, married to a chemical engineer in Silicon Valley."

Turning back to Kat, she continued.

"But she would not have been nearly as happy as she is on the ranch here with Colton—who is a far better man than any I would have chosen. We love him like our own son, Kat, and he treats us with the greatest honor and respect."

"But…" Kat knew what Ling said was true, but couldn't understand how it tied in with her concerns about the baby.

"We have to trust Liu and Colton to make the right decision for their baby," Ling said as her shoulders slumped in defeat. "But I'm with you. And I can't help but feel that the two of them are harboring a secret from the rest of us."

"Another secret?" Kat looked alarmed and then shook her head. "There seem to be a lot of secrets going around West Ranch."

CHAPTER 14

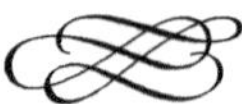

"It's sweet of you to drive me into town, Ridge," Casey said, looking at the snow coming down on the roads. Her husband had a deft hand in navigating the drifts, where her record was not as good.

"Glad to do it," he said, turning to flash her the Ridge West grin she'd fallen in love with a handful of years ago. "I'll drop you off at your office, then I'm meeting Bud Shire for lunch."

"Bud Shire, huh? That sounds like trouble."

"Not at all. We have plenty to talk about, like what he and I are going to wear to the wedding."

Casey laughed.

"I highly doubt that. I hope you're not going to press him for information on the sale of his house, or make him feel bad for not selling it to you, Ridge."

"*Naw*... that's water under the bridge. He's one of my oldest friends—I'm sure he had a perfectly good reason for stabbing me in the back," Ridge said with a wink.

"Play nice," Casey said as she gathered her purse and braced herself to get out at the curb, and walk the ten feet to her office door through blowing snow.

"Would you like to do a little Christmas shopping this afternoon, darlin'?"

"I'm just about done," Casey said. "We got all the girls those beautiful cable-knit sweaters when we were in Ireland, and wool *tam o' shanter* caps and scarves for the guys. We ordered the kids' toys long ago and they're tucked away in our closet—wrapped and ready."

"What about for me?" Ridge asked with a wink. "Do you want a list of suggestions?"

"No, thank you. Your gift is wrapped and ready, too," Casey said with her hand on the door handle, showing Ridge the mischief in her eyes. "Hopefully you won't discover it and ruin the surprise, so stay out of my closet."

Ridge was surprised, she could see.

"Aren't you just keeping me guessing, *Lass*?" Ridge used the nickname and brogue he tried to perfect when they toured Ireland and Scotland recently.

"Aye, Lad," Casey *brogued* back as she leaned over for a kiss. "May the road rise up and greet you… may it hug the tread on your snow tires and keep you safe… and may you remember to bring me a sandwich when you pick me up. Cheers, love."

Ridge laughed heartily and watched his wife until the office door closed firmly behind her. He felt a swell of love for her, and gratitude at the joy she'd restored to his life—it was a different joy than the love he shared with Randi Lynn. With Casey, they were carefree; free to travel and to put each other's needs first.

With the exception of Ash, the boys were now husbands and soon-to-be fathers. They didn't require as much looking after, and to his great pride, he saw them looking after each other. The way it should be.

Even Ash had matured since returning from school. And though Ridge had initial reservations, his relationship with Sassy seemed healthy and strong. He was the one who told Ash that love was a person, not a destination; if Ash decided to follow his girlfriend away from the ranch and to another state, Ridge had no one to blame but himself.

It was like that corny adage about "if you love something, set it free." Ridge loved Ash as much or more than his flesh-and-blood sons. Maybe more, because he needed more love. And if the boy followed Sassy to the end of the earth, why, he and Casey would simply add that location to their travels.

Bud had beat him to the diner and grabbed a corner booth. Instead of a handshake, Bud rose and gave Ridge a bear hug, clapping him heartily on the back. "I guess we're going to be family after all," he said, referencing his daughter Daisy's marriage to Rowdy West.

"I suppose so," Ridge said, signaling the waitress for coffee, "and here you are leaving town. Are you sure you won't change your mind?"

Bud laughed. "I promised my wife sunshine in our retirement, and I aim to keep that promise. She's endured enough Wyoming winters for my career, I suppose. Not to mention emergency calls and late-night prescription refills. All she got for her trouble was one day off a week—remember how the town council nearly hog-tied me when I announced I was closing the drug store on Sundays?"

"I remember," Ridge chuckled, warming with good will at his friend's departure and trying to forgive him for selling the best house in the downtown.

A waitress set down their omelets and refilled their coffee mugs.

"I hear your Casey is retiring, too," Bud said in between bites, "and I know you've been spending more time in Phoenix."

"Yep…" Ridge said his next words carefully. "I know you sold your business to the big guys, and I hear you sold the Craftsman bungalow already, and made a tidy bundle on both. I'm glad you're set up financially, Bud."

Bud set down his fork and looked at his friend.

"I should have asked if you still wanted the house, Ridge. My wife was so excited by the unexpected and generous offer that she agreed for the both of us."

"Can I ask who bought it?"

"You can ask, but it was a lawyer from up near Jackson Hole, representing an unnamed client. I really don't know who bought it, or what they plan on doing with it."

Both men knew that the rich and famous were like locusts; they practically devoured the Jackson Hole area, and were now branching out to Lander, Pinedale and other growing areas of Wyoming.

Ridge sighed in defeat. "Whatever they paid, it was a bargain."

"It will be sad to drive by it when we come back to town," Bud admitted, "but Daisy and Rowdy have a guest suite for us to stay in when we visit. And maybe we'll be so busy with grandchildren that we won't care about the old house."

"Those little ones sure do take the sting off."

CHAPTER 15

"Beef, beef, beef and beef," Daisy said to Paislee. The two were sitting in the office of the West Gorge Arts and Culture Center, opening the RSVPs for the wedding. If everyone showed, it would still be a small affair by many standards, which is how the bride and groom wanted it. "I've heard from just about everyone except my sister."

"I can't believe Darlene hasn't responded to your wedding invitation—and a twin sister to boot. Maybe she's telepathing her reply. Don't twins have their own secret language?"

Daisy laughed at that. "If so, I have a thing or two to telepath to her, words that aren't meant for little ears."

Paislee smiled.

Thankfully, they had been working with a local event planner. With such short notice, the two busy women weren't being stressed beyond their limits. As it was, Paislee had her hands full with the two young kids, and seemed to be a little distant, Daisy thought.

Just a few weeks ago, Paislee had been all *rah rah* about the Culture Center wedding, and the publicity the photos would bring. Still just a blip on the radar of Wyoming brides, they'd be clamoring to be married there once they saw the way her perfect lacy dress popped against the wood and steel beams of the ceiling.

In the summer, the new sandstone walkways would wind around fountains and gardens to a gazebo, where "I do's" could be brilliantly exchanged.

Only now, Paislee wasn't pushing as hard as she was only weeks ago. The "big event" seemed not so big anymore, and Paislee was distracted.

"Daisy, can we talk?" Paislee, whose forehead was lined with some unspoken worry, seemed hesitant, though Daisy was one of her oldest friends.

"Sure, what's up?"

"Are you happy working here—do you like curating exhibits as much as you enjoyed curating for your gallery?"

Daisy set down her pen and notepad and gave the question her full attention.

"I think I like it as much, if not more," Daisy said. "It makes me feel connected to the community, and to the history of the town and people." Then with a laugh, she added, "maybe I'm getting old, but my priorities seem to be shifting away from the latest and greatest, to the past; to artists who documented the west and made history."

Daisy thought about her parents moving to Florida and about her sister disappearing from the face of the earth. How could she bear these losses without the strong love of Rowdy West filling the void?

"I'm glad to hear that," Paislee said with a nod. "Would you consider taking on more hours here? After your wedding and honeymoon, of course."

"Well, I would have to discuss that with Rowdy before answering," Daisy said, slowly. "It's a big step we're taking together, and we're not kids. I'd like to really settle in and turn his big log house into our home, you know. Welcome him at the end of the day with a proper dinner and all. *Beef*, most likely."

Paislee smiled as Daisy talked, and her eyes seemed a little misty as she listened to her friend's dreams, which were about to be realized after so many lonely years.

“I’ve been waiting a long time to be a bride and a wife,” Daisy went on. “The art world, on the other hand, isn’t changing quickly. It can wait for me to come back to it. In fact, I was thinking I might find someone to run Painted Bird Gallery for a time, or maybe just open by appointment until new tourists descend in the spring. My inventory is enough for now, and I can run my online sales from home. Why do you ask?”

Paislee gave her head a shake, as if waking up from a daydream.

“I’ve been thinking similar thoughts, Daisy. It might be time to talk to Kat and the rest of the *Center* board about putting out feelers; finding my replacement. But you are the obvious choice, so I’m floating it by you first.”

“I’m flattered, Paislee. I really am. Not so long ago, it was my dream come true…”

“Until another dream came true.” Paislee said with a tease in her voice. “I didn’t imagine that sending you to Rowdy’s log house all those months ago would result in losing you.”

“Look at it this way,” Daisy said with a smile. “You’re not losing an assistant curator, you’re gaining a cousin.”

CHAPTER 16

"I now pronounce you... husband and wife," the preacher said with delight. "James Timothy, you can kiss your bride."

From the rafters, church bells could be heard ringing throughout the town of Lander; muffled, no doubt, by the softly falling snow.

Sassy squeezed Ash's hand hard as her friend Freda Lang became Freda Freemont, wife of her long-time beau, Jim Tim—the same boy Freda mooned over all summer during the girls' stint at West Ranch.

Freda wore her chestnut hair down, so the butterscotch highlights shone brighter than the stained glass windows of the little white church in the late afternoon sun. Freda's organza dress was surprisingly fashionable for the little town, but after all, they would be local royalty. James Timothy had accepted an entry-level job as an attorney at the DA's office, and Freda would be working for the Wyoming Wildlife Federation.

At the altar, the wedding party was small. Freda's only female cousin stood up with her while wearing a red velvet gown, as James Timothy's brother stood as his best man, complete with a red bowtie. The bride carried a bouquet of white roses and red poinsettias, with sprigs of frosted evergreen boughs. Freda's faux fur stole was at the ready for outdoor photos in the snow.

Tied to each church pew with creamy grosgrain ribbon were more evergreen boughs, and around the church stood tall lanterns with flickering candles.

It was a Christmas wedding straight out of a glossy magazine.

"This is all just perfect," Sassy whispered to Ash as he put his arm around her. There were unshed tears in her eyes when she smiled at Ash, but she couldn't help it. Sassy was overwhelmed with love and joy for her new, but very good friend. "It feels like a fairy tale ending to an unforgettable summer."

"It was unforgettable for me," Ash whispered back, "because I met you."

And fell in love with you.

Ash had yet to say the words that were overflowing from his heart, but felt more than ready. Sassy had promised to stay until Christmas, just two weeks away, and Ash was anxious for answers. Was she going to stay longer—did she love him back? All signs pointed to love, but Sassy was complex and he didn't want to assume, only to wind up with egg on his face.

The attraction and passion between them were growing, that much was undisputable. But these weren't the things that kept a couple together through good times and bad, he knew. And what he wanted more than anything was a family to be true to, forever.

He wasn't about to do anything that would compromise Sassy's honor. Especially since she may not want to be his Wyoming wife.

To Ash, love meant commitment, and commitment meant marriage. And marriage—that meant building a life in West Gorge. That was where the rubber met the road between the two of them. He never wanted to leave Wyoming, and she'd only just arrived. Sassy came for a summer job, and to drop a bombshell on Kat and the West family.

"Come for the internship, stay for the cowboy," he'd once joked, but she didn't take it well—*it's too soon,* she'd told him in no uncertain terms.

To Sassy's credit, she came back to give their relationship a fighting chance, and to see if they could start over with no secrets or expectations between them. Only now, Ash was the one with the secret. He loved the girl like crazy, and desperately wanted her to stay.

"Ready?" Sassy's voice brought him back from wandering. Looking around, Ash could see that they were the last remnant in the pews as everyone else put on coats to make their way to their cars. The dinner reception was being held just a few miles away, but there was no hurry to arrive. Freda told them that they'd be taking their wedding photos in between the ceremony and the reception.

"Hey, wait a minute." Ash took Sassy by the hands, pulling her close to him. "I know you're not the bride, but can I kiss you?"

"In front of God and everyone?" Sassy giggled, glancing around the empty church.

"Sure, why not? I think God approves of love… don't you?"

By answer, Sassy took a step towards Ash and subtly bit her lower lip. He was struck by how beautiful she looked in an evergreen velvet dress. Her hair hung down in buttery curls, with some strands pinned up with crystal-tipped hair pins. Dangling by her jawline, a pair of delicate diamond earrings caught the light and flashed around the little church. The exquisite jewels were an early Christmas gift to Sassy from her sister, Kat.

"Did you say…" Sassy furrowed her brow and tilted her head up to meet Ash's eyes.

"I *love* you, Sassy," Ash said simply.

As Sassy nodded, Ash held his breath, waiting for her rejection. She could turn and walk away from him, he knew, or call him out for pressuring her before she was ready. There were a lot of ways this could go and in Ash's mind, none of them were good. But somehow, by some Christmas miracle, the impossible happened instead.

"I love you too, Ash West."

She really did, he could tell. Their impossibly broad grins and sparkling eyes must have mirrored the other's as they stepped closer. Ash tried to stop smiling so he could bend in and kiss Sassy. His eyes blinked closed and their lips nearly brushed, when a voice interrupted and they jerked away from each other in surprise.

"Well, Jesus loves us all," the wedding preacher said from the aisle.

A skinny man with hallow cheekbones, he was wearing a too-big coat, gloves, and a hat with earmuffs. “But if I don’t lock up and go home for dinner, the missus is going to kill me.”

CHAPTER 17

Ash thought Sassy looked like a princess as they stood by the church's coat rack. He set her velvet winter cape softly over her shoulders and then removed his overcoat from the church hangers—it was the last coat standing. While he buttoned up and tied a muffler around his neck, Sassy carefully placed the cape hood on her head to protect her beautiful hair from the falling snow.

"Ready?" He asked.

"Yes!" Both Sassy and the preacher answered in unison.

Once in the parking lot, he held her arm so her fancy heels would not slip, and guided her to the car. Before opening the door, Ash pulled her close and brought his lips to hers. They stayed together for a long while, until he felt the cold snow freezing the tops of his ears.

"Say it again," Sassy whispered.

"I love you, Sassy Tate," Ash said as he nuzzled his face into the roomy velvet hood.

When at last he pulled away, she smiled at him and said, "we'd better go."

"I know. But you owe me," Ash said, hungry to hear her words one more time—and then a million times more.

They were the last to arrive at the reception and just barely made it before the bride and groom made their entrance. Ash had just enough time to get the two of them a drink from the bar and settle in for dinner, then dancing.

Freda was gracious enough to sit the young couple with her parents and grandparents, in a place of honor. They were close enough to see the love and joy on the bride and groom's faces, especially as they leaned towards each other for several kisses.

"You two are just as beautiful as Freda said," her mother gushed to Sassy as they ate their pecan encrusted salmon, and Hasselback and chive potatoes.

"Thank you, Mrs. Lang," Sassy answered, trying not to look embarrassed. Ash didn't hear—he was busy discussing fly fishing with Freda's grandfather, who placed his hand paternally on Ash's shoulder. The gesture touched Sassy, and made her realize how much Ash depended on the people he placed his trust in, like the men and women of West Ranch—his family.

As for herself, Sassy had a short lifetime of trust with her sweet father and it was enough. It turned out that he wasn't perfect, but he was perfect for her until the time of his passing. Her mother would always be in her life, but Sassy didn't need Sugar Tate on a daily basis. She needed the man sitting next to her. The man who declared his love for her on this lovely winter night.

With sudden hope and clarity, she realized that the next steps were not impossible for the two of them.

The waitstaff began clearing the dinner plates and bringing around pots of coffee and slices of cake. The newlyweds were on the parquet floor for their first dance, followed by the introduction of the parents, grandparents and siblings.

"Now then, let's get all the lovers on the floor, shall we?" The deejay changed the song, and Ash stood to hold his hand out.

"That's us," Ash said with a smile.

In a flash, Sassy recalled the last time they danced, at the West family BBQ. Ash had danced her to a dark corner so she could sob in privacy. She was so relieved to be back in his arms, and at the same time, so weary of carrying such a loaded secret. But all was out in the open now, and Sassy smiled up at the man she loved with all her heart.

"A shadow crossed your beautiful face just now," Ash spoke softly into Sassy's ear as he pulled her into his arms and swayed to the music. "Tell me."

Sassy held his shoulder tighter, and swallowed hard.

"I was thinking about the fight we had last summer, at the BBQ. I was so glad when you came for me and took care of me."

"I'll always take care of you, if you let me," Ash pulled back so she could see his eyes.

"I believe you, Ash."

He thought she had more to say, but she exhaled instead, and rested her face on his shoulder. Pulling her as close as possible, Ash spread his hand on her back and felt the softness of the velvet—it was no match for the creaminess of her skin; this he knew from the one instance when he caught her the first time they met, back when she had altitude sickness.

Ash thought that telling Sassy he loved her, and hearing it in return, would release some of the pent-up emotion and adoration he felt, but it seemed to be multiplying inside his chest instead. He longed to kiss her deeply, and breathe in her love for him.

He needed to put a little distance between them and get back to the table where he could catch his breath.

"*Cake*? Coffee?" Ash quickly let go of a surprised Sassy, and gestured to the table.

LATE THAT NIGHT, THE TWO WALKED UP THE OUTSIDE PINE STEPS OF THE old house-turned-inn. The Lander House Bed and Breakfast had been a lumber baron's Victorian mansion back in the day, and was now fitted with romantic guestrooms and a frilly parlor. They had a master key to get in and keys for their separate rooms down the main hall.

A sign met them at a hall table, telling them where they could find tea and cookies.

"Enjoy the fire and the Christmas tree," the note also said. A silver tree hugged a corner, next to a plush sofa and an antique barrister's bookcase. Twinkling lights lit the room, as did the embers in the fireplace.

"Oh, that's sweet, but I'm so… tired," Sassy managed between yawns.

"Let me walk you to your room."

Sassy looked as though she wanted to protest, but smiled and nodded. She took Ash's hand and he gently pulled her past the welcome desk, a butler's pantry, a room marked ICE, and three other doors with brass room numbers.

"This is me," she whispered, giving her key to Ash. He put the skeleton key in the old oak door and, after a few tries, turned the cut glass knob and swung the door open, taking a quick glance inside before handing the key back.

"Do you want me to check your room for ghosts?"

"Thank you, kind sir," she said, "but no."

Her smile faded just a bit as they looked into each other's eyes. *Ghosts?* They both had plenty of those, Ash thought. But it was easy to push back the pain and insecurity when he was holding this golden girl in his arms. Even better, when they were sitting together and talking as trusted friends.

"I'm right across the hall if you need me," Ash said softly.

"I think that I do need you, Ash West."

Sassy swayed just a little, and Ash smiled at his date. She'd had a glass or two of champagne while he stuck with root beer. He placed one hand on the frame of the door, ready to catch her again if he needed to. With the other hand, he reached down and traced the line of her jaw with his thumb, then steadied her shoulder while he leaned in to kiss her goodnight. She held his eyes until they fluttered softly and closed. He thought his legs might give out from under him.

Her mouth was warm and welcoming and it was hard to pull back. When at last he did, he kissed her gently on both cheeks and stepped away reluctantly.

"I'll stand here until I hear your door lock," he said. "Text me when you're all tucked in."

For a flash, her eyes looked at him with pure desire, but she spun around into the room and pushed the door closed. Hearing the lock click, he sighed and went into his own room. After hanging his suit and brushing his teeth, he splashed handful after handful of cool water on his face and tried to shake the memory of her kiss from taking over his thoughts.

Climbing into the cold sheets, Ash looked over at the text on his phone and groaned.

Miss you already. See you at breakfast. I love you. S

CHAPTER 18

The next morning, Ash sat in front of a frosty bay window looking out at the street. A handful of kids ran by in their snow gear, laughing and pulling sleds. Ash was happy to see that the evergreens on the front lawn of the inn were decorated with oversized red bows and silver balls, and watched as bright red cardinals perched on the snowy boughs.

The snow had stopped falling in the night, thankfully, but more was surely coming and it would be good to get on the road after breakfast.

"Coffee?" A waiter came to the table with a stainless steel carafe, and Ash turned his mug over by way of answer.

Out of the corner of his eye, he could see Sassy walking towards him, wearing a thick white sweater over skinny jeans, and brown leather boots. She wore silver hoop earrings, and a loose sterling silver watch on her wrist. Sassy looked amazing—and all the other men in the room seemed to agree.

Dude, look at your own girl, Ash wanted to scold each man. Instead, he stood and kissed Sassy on the cheek, then pulled her chair out to help her get settled.

"Good morning, beautiful," he said. "Wow, you really look pretty."

With a dull ache in his heart, Ash wished it was their wedding last night; that he'd held Sassy in his arms until daybreak. He wished they'd walked hand in hand down the hall for breakfast, or maybe skipped breakfast altogether.

She smiled at Ash, while turning her mug over for coffee.

"Good morning, Ash," Sassy said with a self-deprecating grin. "Must have coffee. Must have water. I ate a little too much wedding cake last night, and drank a wee bit of the bubbly."

"It was a celebration," Ash said, sipping his coffee, "and you had a designated driver."

"Wasn't it a perfectly wonderful night, Ash? Freda and James Timothy looked so beautiful together and so happy." Sassy sighed as she smiled.

They paused their talking to walk over to the buffet table and fill their plates with toast, fruit and eggs benedict. Ash put a cinnamon roll on his plate too, something Sassy abstained from. While they were at the food table, the waiter filled their mugs with fresh coffee and left two glasses of orange juice.

"Are you sure you don't want a Christmas wedding?" Ash asked as he lifted his fork. He was trying to be casual, even though her answer could completely rock his world. If she said she did, he'd have to wait for a full year to be her husband.

"I don't… I don't want a wedding at all. Not a fan of attention."

"Are you saying… you don't want to be married? Ever?"

"I'd like to be married, Ash, without a public wedding. Does that make sense?"

"You sound like Rowdy. He would have gone to the courthouse in a heartbeat."

"What about you? Do you want a wedding, Ash?"

"As long as it's official, I'm okay with anything."

Sassy nodded.

"Like I told you before," she said, "I can't possibly have a wedding without my sister or my mother, and I can't possibly have both in attendance. It's too much to ask of them, and I love them both. Top that off with my aversion to attention, and it looks like it's the courthouse for me and Mister Right."

"I guess if he's really Mister Right," Ash said, putting cream in his coffee, "he won't care."

"I suppose," Sassy said slyly. "Do you think Mister Right has any demands of his own?"

The corner of Ash's mouth pulled up in a delectable grin, Sassy observed, and she couldn't wait to hear what he had to say.

"Mister Right just hopes for a short engagement—a very. Short. Engagement."

CHAPTER 19

"You look handsome tonight."

Kat West gazed across the table at her husband. They gave the waiter their order and admired the evening view of the frigid lake from their window seats. A few homes on the far shoreline glowed with Christmas lights in their windows, and twinkling pine trees by their docks. This was Kat's favorite season to visit this restaurant.

The posh log inn was beautifully decorated itself, with red and green lights on a trim pine tree, and roaring logs in a stone fireplace.

On the table, a flickering candle in a lantern cast a romantic light on Gunnar's rugged face. Kat enjoyed seeing her man in a sport coat every now and then, instead of the thick canvas and denim ranching clothes. She thought that secretly he enjoyed it too. Gunnar had a closet full of tailored suits, silk ties and linen button-down shirts just dying to come out and play.

Remembering back on their first date, Kat pegged the cowboy as someone who wouldn't know fine dining if it bit him on the butt. As it turned out, Gunnar was far more sophisticated than she could have guessed. Not only was he a board member of the hospital where she worked, but he had his MBA, and was a major benefactor to the town.

In her defense, he'd bucked the quarantine like a wild bull when she informed him that he was stuck in her hospital lock down. But soon, he began to pitch in and ease the tense situation for everyone. At the same time, she started to see how much pain he was in over the loss of his mother. The two began to work together, which lead to admiration and then love.

"Cheers, Kat," Gunnar said, lifting his goblet of sparkling cider. Kat declined anything stronger since she had an early morning meeting at the hospital, and Gunnar followed suit.

"Cheers, darling," she answered, and took a sip. "I'm *starved* tonight. You'd better guard your steak—I'll eat all of mine and half of yours if you don't."

Gunnar grinned broadly and covered her hand with his. He remembered telling Ridge that he wanted to meet a woman with an appetite—for love, life, and for everything. That was the night he met Kat, and his life changed forever.

"You're so beautiful tonight in that itty bitty silk dress, I'll give you anything you want. Speaking of which, what's on your Christmas list this year, doc?"

"Oh, the usual. Peace on earth. Goodwill toward men. A new hospital wing for the infectious disease department."

As Gunnar laughed at his wife's comment, the waiter set down their salads and rolls.

"I see how it is. And here I thought this was purely social."

Kat smiled back. "I'm just teasing. We can talk about the new wing in the new year."

"Then let's get back to Christmas."

Already buttering her second roll, Kat pondered the question while chewing.

"I think you and I should take a trip this winter, someplace warm. We can leave Willow with Liu and Colton for a few weeks. The Chen's love her so much, and with six adults under their roof, they'll surely get her to school and back every day."

"Done. But Santa can't wrap a vacation and put it under the tree, Kat."

"Tell Santa there's a stunning opal bracelet at Dee's Jewelers downtown. The stones are local, and the silver setting is to die for."

"I hope it's still there when Santa can get to town," Gunnar said.

"It will be," Kat said slyly. "Dee has it tucked away in the back, with your name on it."

The waiter brought their steaks and refilled their goblets as the two nodded their thanks.

"I suppose you want to know what's on my Christmas list," Gunnar said.

"Actually, no. I already have your present. It's all wrapped up and everything," Kat said.

Gunnar lifted his eyebrows in surprise as he chewed his perfectly seasoned Porterhouse.

"Well well," he said, gazing admirably at his super busy wife. Not only did she head up a busy hospital department, but she was a fabulous mother, the perfect wife, and head of the charitable foundation his mother started. "When did you find the time?"

"Months ago," Kat said, mysteriously. She set down her fork and steak knife and reached for his hand. "I love you so much, Gunnar West."

He gave her his full attention. Tears were pooling in her eyes and about to spill. Reaching into his pocket, he handed Kat a clean handkerchief to dab her eyes.

"Are you okay?" He spoke softly, while squeezing her hand. All Kat could do was nod.

"How is it," she managed, "that you can be married to a man for nearly seven years, only to realize over dinner how much you really love him?"

"Love grows. And when you least expect it, it takes your breath away," Gunnar said through a lump in his throat. "I speak from first-hand experience."

Kat laughed softly and looked away from his eyes and towards the fire, so she could regain her countenance and finish her dinner. She saw the waiter approach their table but Gunnar subtly waved him off. As she took long, slow breaths, Kat thought back to summer, when

Sassy was interning at the ranch and guarding a secret that would rock everyone's world. After Gunnar intervened, forcing her to face the truth head-on, their marriage was bruised and battered—she wondered if the damage was permanent. But with a little perspective, she could see that he always had her best interests at heart.

Looking up at last, Kat saw her husband regarding her with such devotion and kindness, she was overwhelmed with another flood of love and desire for the man she'd married—the man she almost allowed to get away.

"Bit of a wreck tonight," Kat attempted, while holding her fork with a trembling hand.

"You're never, ever, that," Gunnar said definitively. "You are remarkable."

Kat sniffed.

"Now then, Sheriff," Gunnar continued after changing to a more upbeat tone. "I suggest we order a third steak, another bottle of cider, and two slices of German chocolate cake. We still need to talk about what Santa is going to bring Willow this Christmas."

"And," Kat brightened, "all the *secrets* floating around the ranch!"

CHAPTER 20

"Do you think you're being a bit... paranoid?"

Gunnar held Kat's coat as they got ready to head back home—a valet was retrieving Gunnar's truck. He would have liked to take his wife out in a sportier car, but the snow was falling and roads were slick.

"Hah," Kat laughed. "You know what they say, just because you're paranoid, it doesn't mean they're *not* out to get you."

Gunnar laughed and pulled his wife into a hug. He enjoyed their nights on the town. Kat was always a lively conversationalist—something he got precious little of on the day-to-day ranch operation. Out on the range, he and the other cowboys talked about the livestock and building maintenance. But with his wife, they covered a wide range of topics, from diseases to travel destinations; from recipes to world events. And apparently, conspiracy theories.

"Let's establish that nobody is out to get you, Kat West," he said.

"I know, but people are being cagey. It's funny, but besides you, the person I trust the most these days is Sassy. Not long ago she was public enemy number one, but she's been so open and honest. And don't let this get around, but I really am growing to love having a little sister."

"She always reminded me of you," Gunnar said. "I hope she sticks around."

"Well, we can discuss that topic."

"Let's put a pin in that and get back to everyone else... like Dad, for instance. You don't really think he's hiding anything, do you?"

"There's *something* Ridge and Casey aren't telling us, that's for sure. Pike and Paislee also have a secret. If little Ford were older, I could ply him with chocolate milk until he talked, but all he knows is that Santa is bringing his toys to the ranch this year, and not their house."

"Paislee's explanation sounded good."

"Too good, if you ask me," Kat said, "but not believable. Paislee loves decorating for Christmas, and she's being a bit secretive. And did you see how they avoided the topic when we were trimming the tree?"

"Yeah, I caught that. Who else?" Gunnar slipped his arms into his overcoat and placed the leather cowboy hat on his head—the one Kat thought was low-class on their first date. She had no idea that it cost as much as some guys spend on their first car.

"Liu and Colton are keeping something from us, and I can't imagine what it is."

"It's a West family conspiracy, from the sounds of it." Gunnar took his wife's arm and kept her steady as they walked outside to their truck. The valet held Kat's door open until Gunnar slipped him a large bill. "I'll take it from here," he told the young man. He wanted to have a minute with Kat, to take her in his arms under the falling snow and full moon; to kiss her good and proper before they went back to their regularly scheduled life.

He wasted no time.

"Wow... what was that?" Kat's knees felt weak, but Gunnar's arm around her was strong.

"Just a reminder that I'm crazy about you, and that I'm not keeping any secrets. I'm an open book."

Her smile was radiant. Even with their heavy coats between them, Gunnar felt her fall against him without reserve. She was all in, Kat West was, and loved him without holding anything back.

"Do you know what I love about you?" He asked her as he gently kissed sparkling ice crystals off her eyelids, and tenderly brushed the cold flakes from the waves of her hair.

"What's that?"

"You're not afraid of a little snow."

Back in the restaurant, two valets and the host stood near a frosty window, gazing at the smitten couple by the entrance who had their arms around each other, and couldn't seem to stop kissing and laughing. They didn't seem in any hurry to get in the truck.

"Why they paid me a fortune to bring the truck 'round, only to stand outside in a blizzard, I'll never know," the one valet said to the other.

"Crazy," the other one said, wishing he'd been the one to get the old pickup.

CHAPTER 21

"Here's the last of my things; there's no turning back now, cowboy," Daisy said, standing inside Rowdy's warm log home. He set down the final box from the back of Daisy's car, and stood straight and tall again to catch his breath. Rowdy had worked fast to minimize his exposure to the cold and snow.

"I would hope you weren't planning on turning back," he said with a breathy smile as he leaned in for a kiss. "Our wedding is a week away."

Her smile held a little tease, as she stood barefoot in his foyer wearing a long-sleeved tee shirt and faded jeans. Rowdy was happy to see her looking so at home in his home, and counted the days until the sight of her welcoming him would be routine. It was such a simple pleasure to be welcomed home, but one that had eluded him—unless he counted his brother Gray, which just seemed kind of depressing.

"Mmm, you taste like winter and fresh air," she said appreciatively, holding his cold face with her warm hands.

Still in his suede leather coat and wool scarf, Rowdy wrapped his arms fully around Daisy's waist and lifted her off the ground.

"Oh, hello," she managed to say, dangling from his arms.

Still breathing hard from the cold wind and the exertion of quickly unpacking her car, Rowdy squeezed her tight and kissed her with a passion he was finding harder to keep under wraps. Responding in kind, she matched his kiss and raised the ante by running her hands through his thick, snowy curls.

"One more week," Rowdy whispered in her ear as he smiled with appreciation and gently lowered Daisy, "and then I plan on being a very, married man."

"No one will be happier for you, sir, than me," Daisy said with a small laugh and curtsey. "Now, I plan on going into the bedroom—and you should probably not come with me. I'm going to unpack some of these boxes, if you cleared a space for me in the closet."

"Take as much as you want." Rowdy hung up his coat, then traded his boots for wool slippers before padding to the kitchen for a cup of hot coffee. "It's all yours, or it soon will be. You will find me a very easy roommate. And if you don't like this house, we'll find another—or get on Colton's waiting list, and he can build us a custom home."

Daisy looked surprised.

"This is a beautiful home, Rowdy," she said. "It suits you, and you suit me. And there aren't many homes in town with a view of the mountains like this one has."

Taking each other's hand, they went to sit on the leather sofa facing the fireplace and tall picture windows. Once Rowdy was settled, Daisy curled up next to him and pulled a wool throw over her chilled legs. He had his coffee in one hand and wrapped the other arm around his soon-to-be bride.

"I imagine we'll have many winter nights, curled up like this," she said.

"I'm counting the minutes, Daisy." Rowdy kissed the top of her head, then took a sip from his ceramic Painted Bird Gallery mug. "The second you walked into this house I knew you belonged here with me. If you brought a preacher with you that day, I would have married you right then and there."

"What was I thinking, not bringing a preacher with me to help you choose paintings for your walls?" Her small rippled laugh quickly turned into another yawn. "I just might have married you, though. As it is, I thought you'd never ask."

"Really? I thought I was rushing things."

"The minute you opened the door, I knew you were the one I'd been waiting for."

Rowdy squeezed her again.

"How much more do you need to bring over from your house?"

"Nothing. That's it," Daisy said. "Since I'm keeping my house as a vacation rental, I left the beds and bedding, towels, and a fully stocked kitchen. I packed my clothes and valuables and cleared out the clutter. I replaced my original oil paintings with inexpensive framed photos, though. Now there's nothing in the house I really care about. It's all right here." Daisy looked up at Rowdy, before settling her head heavily against him once more.

"I'm all in," she said sleepily, then closed her eyes.

Rowdy moved his hand slowly up and down Daisy's back as her breathing slowed. In minutes, she was breathing evenly. *Sleep, sweet one,* he whispered, taking another sip of coffee. He reached down to the blanket that covered her legs, and pulled the corner up to her shoulder.

Love was simple acts of caring, he thought. It was trust.

He'd only been dating Daisy for a few months, but trusted her enough to open his life up to her. He opened a generous bank account in her name, deeded her the house, and took out a life insurance policy that would keep her warm for all her days—none of which she knew yet. She was a blessing to him from God, at a time in his life when he figured he might be destined for loneliness. She said that she was all in, and so was he.

In his early forties, Rowdy knew children may or may not be in their future; either way, he would honor Mrs. Daisy Shire West until death parted them.

Some of Rowdy's ancestors were coming to the end of their full lives by the time they reached his age, he knew. Kin of Pickford West, the ones that followed him from Pennsylvania to Wyoming and then Montana in the 1800's, were married with children before the age of twenty, and grandparents by forty. They toiled and strained and gave their bodies to tame the land they loved, to leave a legacy for the last Wests standing in Montana.

Rowdy had started to think of himself as an old guy, ready for pasture. But moving to Wyoming and working alongside Gunnar gave him a new purpose. He had a hope for the future since meeting the fresh and vibrant Daisy.

"Mmm," Daisy mumbled in her sleep as she burrowed against Rowdy for warmth.

He felt a flood of love and devotion warm him—it worked its way up to his throat, where it formed a lump of unfamiliar emotion that was almost painful. At the same time, a sense of panic crept up from the pit of his stomach and gripped his heart.

What was he doing, marrying such a lovely girl? He, a grizzled rancher with a bum leg, and little experience in the ways of keeping a woman interested. He'd proven that.

"Easy boy," he whispered to himself as he slowly exhaled, releasing the anxiety. Her love was pure and sweet, without guile. If she was fooling him then so be it, Rowdy figured. He'd take his lumps. But if his instincts were right, there were only good days ahead."

"I love you, Rowdy," came the sleepy mumble from Daisy's sweet lips as she stirred.

"Shh," he hushed, "I love you too, Daisy."

With his hand on her shoulder, he squeezed her and smiled.

CHAPTER 22

"What are you doing in these parts, cowboy?"

Sassy smiled at Ash when she opened the door of her apartment and kissed the tall handsome visitor on the lips. Ash removed his hat and coat, and wiped the snow off his boots. It was early evening and he'd had an errand in town.

"Didn't you get my text?"

"No I..." Sassy looked around for her phone, which was nowhere to be found. "I must have left my phone at the desk of Amber Waves. I was helping out for an hour after work today. Amber is starting to mark down her inventory for a pre-Christmas sale, and the ladies are going nuts."

"I thought I saw Wayne running around like a chicken when I walked through the store."

"Just be glad Amber didn't see you—she would have roped you in. Coffee?"

Ash smiled as Sassy went to her kitchen island. The little room was like a one-room cabin on the prairie, though a bit bigger. By the lead-glass street front windows stood a tall built-in bookcase, a long sofa, and an antique oak rocking chair. There was a coffee table and a side table for a lamp.

In the middle of the room, a kitchen island was flanked by appliances and cupboards.

On the other side of the room, looking like a picture in a catalog, was a brass bed. Sassy had a fluffy down comforter spread over the top, with thick downy pillows leaning against the headboard. A folded wool throw sat at the foot, ready to warm cold toes.

Ash pulled his eyes away from the bed, before his imagination began to wander to what it would be like to wake up under that downy comforter on a cold morning. The cozy room had everything one person could need. Maybe two people, if that second person brought only one change of clothes and a toothbrush.

"Here you go," Sassy said as Ash walked to the sofa. "I just brewed a fresh pot."

"I see you got some new mugs from Amber's store," Ash said with a smile.

"Yes, I did, thanks to my employee discount. Merry ChrisMoose, Ash. I'll just run down and grab my phone. Be right back."

Ash sat down on Sassy's sofa with his coffee and glanced at her laptop, which she'd left open. He didn't mean to spy, but the page she'd been working on looked like a job application. After he heard her door close, Ash lifted the computer and brought it closer—indeed it was an application for an accounting firm... in Chicago.

Availability? Immediate, the form said.

Sassy was leaving.

The blood drained out of Ash's head as his thoughts swirled like a twister. How could she leave—how could that be? They had a meaningful wedding weekend in Lander where they confessed their love for each other. They stood in the church, and under the falling snow, and in the hallway of the old inn and said their "I love you's."

Did that mean nothing to Sassy? It sure meant everything to Ash. It was the moment he'd been waiting so patiently for; the foundation to build their life on.

Every nerve in Ash's body told him to run. *Get up and storm out,* his head told him as the adrenaline surged through his veins; *grab your coat and go.* Instead, he stayed put. Storming out is what he did in the summer when the two were beginning to date, and it hadn't gone well. He learned… they both learned… that honest conversations were better for a relationship than emotional reactions. As much as he was hurting, he'd wait and hear what she had to say.

Surely, he misunderstood what he was seeing, for Sassy wouldn't just up and leave him now… would she?

"Hey, sorry that took so long. I had to ring up a woman before she blew a gasket."

As Ash set the laptop back on the coffee table and looked up, Sassy could see that he was stricken by what he saw. She came next to him and sat down.

"I'm sorry for snooping," Ash said, "but it looks like you're applying for a job in Chicago."

Ash sat back and waited for Sassy to clear up the misunderstanding.

"I was going to tell you. A recruiter called and asked me to apply to one of the biggest accounting firms in the Midwest—isn't that great? It's entry level, but their client roster is a dream. I hoped my grades were good enough and it seems I was right."

"Wow, I don't know what to say, except congratulations."

Ash felt like a robot, saying words he knew he ought to say. He tried not to sound cold and distant, but he was so confused about what that meant for him—for the two of them. His heart was pounding with a dull, painful thud as he wondered how quickly he could leave without seeming like a petulant child.

Sassy watched him closely, and chose her next words carefully.

"I told them I was available right now, because you always say that on applications," she gave a little laugh, "at least you do when you're just starting out, right?"

"Right," Ash said dully.

"But I'm sure they won't want me to start until after the holidays at this point."

Right.

Ash meant to say the word, but had run out of steam. Sassy Tate, the girl he'd given his heart to, was going to leave. He couldn't fault her. She'd kept her word and stayed through December, but then she was going back home to Illinois.

Merry ChrisMoose to me, Ash thought sadly as he got up and grabbed his coat and hat, then closed her door softly behind him.

CHAPTER 23

"Hey, why don't you kids go and play in Willow's room?"

At the ranch, Pike and Paislee nervously followed Kat and Gunnar, and Ridge and Casey, into the great room to sit by the fire. Gunnar carried a tray with mugs and creamer, while Kat brought the carafes of coffee.

The kids, who had been screaming and laughing as they ran back and forth in front of the large Christmas tree, chased each other down the hall to play with toys.

It was just days before Santa's arrival, and both Kat and Paislee were showing signs of weariness as the little ones were nearly frantic at the impending arrival of the jolly old elf. It was all the young moms could do to keep them busy enough during the day to finally fall asleep each night.

"Those pork chops were amazing, Casey," Kat said, complimenting the cook. "Thank you for a beautiful dinner."

"Yes, thank you, Casey," Paislee and the men chimed in. "I'm glad we all could get together on such short notice, because Pike and I…"

She trailed off and looked to her husband with terror and exhaustion in her eyes, Kat could see. He nodded at her, and sat forward in his chair.

"You see, we have some news." Pike exhaled and looked around at his family. "We are going to Denver after Christmas."

"We knew that," Gunnar said. "You always visit your Colorado family at Christmas."

"Only this time," Paislee said, "it's not a visit—we're not coming back."

"You... what?" Kat was shocked, as was Gunnar, Ridge and Casey.

"We are moving our lives to Denver. Starting with the new year, the children will attend the private school I went to," Paislee explained. "We are going to live in the Andrews mansion with my mother and father, and grandmother Gigi. Since my sisters moved into their own homes, there's more than enough room. It's time to let my family get to know Sun and Ford more intimately than they do."

Kat thought Pike and Paislee looked miserable. This was the secret they'd been keeping, and for good reason. Their two children were Willow's cousins and playmates. But it made sense, she couldn't deny that.

"What about your studio, Pike?" Gunnar was concerned for his brother, who hid his talents and desires for years, only to finally be living his dream as an artist.

"Pepper, Paislee's mother, is turning the property's carriage house into a studio for me," Pike said with a smile.

"She's so excited to have us come to stay." Paislee couldn't hide her happiness, which quickly turned to sorrow and tears, they could all see. "Although it means leaving West Ranch and everyone here. Which is so much harder than I ever expected."

"We grew on you Paislee, I knew we would," Ridge got up and pulled Pike into a lengthy bear hug, and then gave a very tender hug to his son's heiress bride. He kissed his daughter-in-law on the cheek and wiped a lone tear from his face.

Soon, everyone was standing and hugging each other as the realization set in.

"What am I going to do without you, Paislee?" Kat sat down, mouth open in shock.

"The good news is," Paislee smiled weakly as she also sat back down, “we will back when school is out to spend our summers in Wyoming.”

“We will be keeping our house in West Gorge Woods as our summer residence,” Pike said. “Colton will keep an eye on it while we’re gone; we stopped to see them on our way here, since they couldn’t join us tonight.”

“Liu looks miserable,” Paislee said quietly to Kat, “and I know she’s past her due date.”

“I’m a little miserable myself,” Kat tried to smile as she reached for Paislee’s hand. “You were my first sister, Paislee. Before Liu, before Casey, and even before my own sister, Sassy. I’m going to miss you so much. And I don’t know how I’m going to tell Willow. But I understand.”

Tears were flowing freely down everyone’s faces when the three children ran back in the room and took in the scene. The little ones froze, as Ford spoke his worst fear.

“Did you get bad news Mommy,” he asked. “Is Santa Claus cancelling Christmas?”

CHAPTER 24

"We missed another chance to tell them our news."

Casey turned down the warm comforter on their bed in the ranch, and opened the curtains so they could see the mountains and gorge come into view with the early morning light. The snow had been picking up, however, and it might be a white-out by sunrise. They'd want to see that, too.

"I know, I know," Ridge said, taking off his wristwatch and admiring his wife in her body-hugging pajamas. It felt like just yesterday when he and Casey were climbing trees together to get a look at leaky roofs, and other such antics as real estate rivals. He'd still help her down from trees and rescue her from blizzards if that's what it took to be near her. Tonight, as the wind blew snow against the windows, he was happy for the simple joy of warm flannel sheets, and his lovely wife.

"I didn't have the heart, after seeing how heartbroken Kat was to find out about Pike and Paislee leaving Wyoming," he said. "And so soon after Christmas."

Casey nodded, slipping between the sheets. Resting her head on the down pillow, she looked over at Ridge who was about to do the same. She never got over the thrill of seeing her handsome husband smile at her the way he did each night—the look on his face was nothing short of mischievous as he reached for her with obvious delight.

"We can't just send everyone a postcard..." Casey attempted, smiling as Ridge slowly kissed her neck and jawline.

"*We...*" Ridge said in a low and grumbly voice that rippled down Casey's spine like a summertime creek over rocks, "we can do whatever we want, Casey girl."

For the most part, he was right.

Nothing much changed in the first years of their marriage. Casey and Ridge were happy carrying on with the lives each had built. Ridge attended town leadership meetings and helped drive the growth and development of West Gorge. He met other business leaders for breakfasts, and popped into the ranch offices every now and again.

Now, Ridge left the matters of the town to his grown sons.

"Allocate West land as you see fit," he told Gunnar, Pike, Colton and Ash. "Build the town you want your children to be proud of."

With Bud Shire moving away, the breakfasts were fewer, and frequented by the old-timers, which made Ridge feel ancient. The town's younger leaders didn't *do* breakfast. They had text chains and private Facebook groups; they held remote Zoom meetings, and met for thirty minute "power lunches."

The changes had been gradual, but Ridge found he was happier having breakfast with Casey, and riding horses with his grandchildren instead of running the town.

As for Casey, she kept working at first. She had wanted to prove that she could provide for herself, still, even though she'd married a very wealthy man—until little by little, she let her guard down. As her trust grew, she realized it was more important to be with Ridge than to keep her business going.

She began to sell off properties. With each house sold, it was like letting go of a stronghold, something that held her, and she found it freeing. Before long, she was able to take the remnant of her business, the property management services, and just hand it to her competitor —who happened to be Amber and her boyfriend, Wayne.

Amber, who she'd trained since high school, in turn taught Wayne the ins and outs of the business. By the time he was ready to hang his shingle, Casey was ready to retire hers.

"Here you go, Wayne," she told him, handing him the biggest slice of real estate pie he'd ever not worked for. "Have fun with this, and take care of our girl."

Wayne gladly agreed. "I'll take good care of Amber, and the business. I promise."

CHAPTER 25

"Do you smell that storm coming in?"

Ridge sat with Ash at Cindy's diner, enjoying a rare bit of time together. It was three days until Christmas, and the restaurant was draped in silver tinsel and shining red ornaments. The waitresses were wearing fur-trimmed Santa hats, and everyone seemed to be in a happy mood—even the cash register sounded festive as it jingled with coins.

"I smell snow…" Ash said, "I smell eggs and bacon. But I don't smell a storm."

"Smell it or not, here it comes," Ridge said with a laugh as Cindy set their breakfasts down and gave him a sideways glance. "Give yourself a few years as a rancher and you'll be able to smell storms in the air, too."

Ash picked up a piece of his bacon and let his shoulders drop.

"Unless I move to Chicago with Sassy, and walk away from the ranch altogether."

"If you do that, son," Ridge said, "you'll have to own that decision and make the best of it. Not make her feel guilty, or walk around with your head hanging down like a sad puppy."

Ash nodded.

"Can I ask you something, Dad?" Ash looked into Ridge's eyes. "Did your first wife, Randi Lynn, have an issue with moving from Michigan to Wyoming, or did she make a clean break?"

"*Hoo hoo,* no it was not a clean break."

Ridge set his fork down and gave the question his full attention. "The decision was impulsive, as was our marriage, and she may have repented a little through the years. Randi Lynn was a hotshot lawyer in Detroit, and traded everything she knew for a much different life. She traded her career for the ranch and for motherhood—and for *me.* She traded civilization for small town living; for gossipy women who made it hard for her to fit in. She gave up high fashion, social-climbing parties, and happy hours for dusty horses, dusty men and a dusty, dirty old town filled with scratchy clothes and durable boots."

Ash listened closely to his dad as he said words he'd never heard before, and may never hear again.

"Randi Lynn also walked clean away from her home and family in northern Michigan, and rarely saw her kin. They were so angry at her for giving up her promising career, and sure she'd made a big mistake in marrying me instead of the tall Finnish lawyer they had their eye on." Ridge laughed a little as he looked out the window, deep in his memories. "That just made her more determined, if you ask me."

"Determined?" Ash asked, hoping for more insight.

"Yep, Randi Lynn attacked motherhood, ranching and West Gorge like a boss. She invited the town women over one by one and in groups, until she became not only accepted, but the leader of the pack. She ran our home and ranch like a corporation and let me tell you, we towed the line for fear of being fired." Ridge chuckled at a private thought.

"She made it clear to me that she and I were partners. That whatever arrangement previous West men had with their wives was off the table—she and I would make decisions together regarding our sons, our property and our town. Which had become her town."

Ridge looked back at Ash and tilted his head for his final words.

"She made me a better man, Ash," he said. "I didn't see it at the time, only in the rear-view mirror."

"Are you saying..."

"Ash, I'm not saying anything. You and Sassy need to make your own decisions about your future. But I'm proud of you for going slow; for stepping back and allowing your relationship to take its sweet time."

"I just wish I could have both West Ranch, *and* Sassy Tate," Ash sighed in defeat, spreading a little jam on his toast.

"You're assuming a lot, Son. Can't you have both?" Ridge's question caused Ash to look up and take notice. "It seems to me, Ash, you think you have your answer, when you haven't even asked the question."

CHAPTER 26

"Good old West Gorge, Wyoming. It hasn't changed a bit, has it?"

Darlene Shire looked around her parents' barren living room as she perched on the hard floor of the Craftsman bungalow. The trademark built-in book cases sat empty and gleaming, and the oak pillars that divided the living room from the dining room shone with polished wood grain. Ancient oak details also defined other features of the one-of-a-kind home—such as a trayed ceiling, paneled walls and thick window casements.

Snow beat against the lead glass transoms and rattled the tight little house, causing the fireplace flames to flicker as wind traveled down the stone chimney. As she looked up, the lit mission-style light fixtures dimmed momentarily, and Darlene held her breath. Being home was depressing enough with the power on; if it went out altogether, she might get the excuse she'd been looking for to avoid her sister's wedding.

The movers had already packed up the boxes of books, china, and linens, along with the heirloom furniture pieces, and sent them ahead to the Shire's new detached condo in Florida. The beds and a few last boxes would be picked up by the town's charity store after the Shire's left the house to the new owner.

Two days before the wedding, the family's final lunch together in the Shire house consisted of a few pizzas and sodas as they perched on flattened cardboard. The fireplace kept the room as cozy as possible while Darlene sat with her parents, her twin sister Daisy, and Rowdy West—who looked disturbingly like her former beau, Gunnar.

In fact, Darlene thought, as she nibbled and gazed over her pizza at the couple, the two could pass as the actors hired to play herself and Gunnar in her made-for-TV biography; titled, no doubt, *So Many Regrets: The Darlene Shire Story.* The story of a girl who nearly married into local royalty, only to throw it all away for a career in journalism, then wound up selling shoes in a California strip mall.

Darlene wished she could go back and marry into the wealthy West family, who would have been glad to see her divorce Gunnar, and take her hefty settlement with her as she left town.

Her life would be much different, she knew, if only she'd been a little more patient. By the time she figured out her mistake and came back to accept Gunnar's lukewarm proposal, that wily doctor had locked him up tight in the hospital and convinced him he loved *her* instead.

She thought for sure the marriage would crumble in the first few years; so much so that she searched online almost weekly for *Gunnar West Divorce*—only to get photos of he and his wife, Kat, cozying up to each other at charity events, hospital galas and fundraising dinners. They looked somewhat happy, Darlene grudgingly observed, noting that Kat West had a growing collection of diamonds and other jewels.

"Actually, the little town has changed a lot," Bud Shire contradicted his daughter. "The new Arts and Culture Center is wonderful, and we have a brand new cancer center in town—all thanks to the West family."

Bud nodded at Rowdy as he said this.

"Your father's little drug store will soon be a big box pharmacy on the edge of town," Darlene's mother said with obvious pride, "with restaurants on either side, and a party supply store."

"And don't forget Amber Waves downtown," Bud offered, "and several new houses going up in West Gorge Woods..."

"All right, *all right,* I get it," Darlene said, sourly, as her parents shared a look. Bud and his wife had been glad when Darlene left town, and had been tempted to change the locks on the bungalow.

At their new place in Florida, they would welcome Daisy and Rowdy anytime they wanted to visit, but were considering finding a nearby hotel in the event that Darlene showed up—she had a tendency to become a wee bit entrenched, and their sheltering days were over.

Rowdy was the perfect gentleman, Darlene had to admit, as he made light conversation and asked about her life in California. He nodded agreeably as she painted a rosy picture. She could see that he was quite smitten with Daisy as he reached for her hand several times, and caught her eyes as they all talked. Rowdy even pretended to be interested in her parents' boring travel plans, and in the amenities at their new home association.

"Tennis courts and three swimming pools," her mother gushed, "one just for laps."

"They have a weekly potluck dinner and there's always someone to play cards with," her dad said with a smile.

The wind blew a powerful gust against the windows, and the lights flickered once again as everyone looked at each other with trepidation.

"And sunshine," her mother said weakly, "lots and lots of sunshine."

Just then, nearly everyone in the room was startled by loud alerts clanging on their cell phones, and looked at the small screens.

"Flights are going to be cancelled, beginning later this evening," Darlene said, dourly, "until indefinitely—next week, maybe."

"Roads are going to be closed by morning," Bud Shire said to his wife and family. "With this storm, it could be a week until the plows are able to get out."

"The courthouse is closing early today," Rowdy told Daisy. "They may not open tomorrow as planned, so if we want to get our license, we better go now."

Daisy looked around the room at her family, new and old, and smiled. She'd had the blessing of seeing her parents nearly every day of her life, and knew she would miss them when they moved. But their joy and happiness dulled that pain as she looked at their excited faces.

Her sister, Darlene, had also blessed her by making the trip for the wedding, and to meet her husband-to-be. Her twin had chosen a circuitous, miserable journey for herself in life, and Daisy often tried to correct her course, with no luck. While she would always love her twin, Darlene had to find her own way, and live with her unfortunate decisions.

Rowdy West was Daisy's future. In this room full of her loved ones, he was the one she wanted to go home with and build a life with. At that moment, nothing else mattered.

"Then let's go to the courthouse," Daisy said with a bright smile.

CHAPTER 27

"Merry Christmas Eve, *eve*!"

"Same to you, what's wrong, Kat? You sound stressed."

Sassy answered her sister's call on the first ring, and didn't like the tone in Kat's voice.

"I am on pins and needles, Sass..." Kat said. "Can you pack your bag and come to the ranch? I think I need you here, and your room is always ready."

"Yeah, sure. I was going to come tomorrow after the wedding anyway, but if you need me, I'll come now," Sassy said, secretly glad to be needed by her big sister—the one she didn't know existed until a year ago.

"It's your first Wyoming winter, and this storm could keep us all in place for days, or weeks. I'd feel better if you were stuck here, instead of in town."

"Okay, but what about..." Sassy was thinking out loud, but heard what Kat said, loud and clear. "Never mind. I'm nearly packed anyway, so I'll be there soon. Love you."

These words were new to the sisters, and she hoped the sentiment would be returned. The phone was silent for a beat.

"I love you to, Sass," Kat said, "be careful on the road, and don't wait too long. Please."

A blast of snow and wind hit the window and pulled her out of her thoughts as she sprang into action. Her gown from Freda's wedding was still hanging in her car from the dry cleaners, along with a new champagne-colored velvet gown her mother graciously sent for Rowdy and Daisy's wedding. Her suitcase was half packed with warm sweaters and jeans for Christmas day, and a few pair of flannel pajamas, plus her coziest fleece slippers.

Her Christmas gifts were wrapped and under the tree at the ranch already. And Ash West was there, working hard to secure the ranch in the storm. What more did she need?

On her way through the twinkling store with bags in hand, Sassy informed Amber that she had to be with her family and couldn't help with the sale. Looking around, she could see there were no customers, which made her feel a little better about ditching her friend on the last shopping day before Christmas.

"Everyone's staying home, so I'm about to close up anyway until the new year," Amber told her. "You'd better get out of here before you get snowed in with me and Wayne."

"Ugh," Sassy joked, hugging her friend. "Merry Christmas, Amber."

"Merry Christmas, Sassy," Amber said with a tear in her eye. "You've been a good friend, helping me so much."

Sassy wiped away her own tear and laughed, "I'm just going a few miles down the road to the ranch. It's not like I'm leaving town."

"You better not," Amber said, shutting the door hard behind Sassy and watching to make sure she got her car out of the snowy drift she was parked in. She could see her friend fishtail in the fresh layer, but then straighten out. When Amber could no longer see Sassy's tail lights on the road, she flipped her store sign to CLOSED, and exhaled.

CHAPTER 28

"Liu is in labor!"

Colton called Kat, who was watching the storm from the safety and warmth of the ranch.

"Thank goodness you two were at my condo," Kat told him. "Just in time."

"Agreed. The Chens are staying there now. They should be able to navigate the short distance to the hospital when it's time, even in this storm. Thanks for your hospitality, Kat."

"Of course, Colton. Give Liu my love, and tell the Chens to make themselves at home. There's plenty to eat, and a backup generator will keep the condo warm and the lights on, even if the power goes out in town."

"Good to know," Colton said. "I'll keep you posted, and leave it to you to inform everyone else. I don't want to be away from Liu for long. I still can't believe I'm going to be a father."

Kat smiled and felt her throat constrict.

"You'll be awesome," she managed in a throaty whisper.

After hanging up, Kat sent out a group text and then went to make a fresh pot of coffee in the kitchen. It was going to be a long night. She said a quick prayer of gratitude that Liu had finally dropped her stubborn resistance and moved closer to town before going into labor.

Gazing out the window at the storm, it was easy to imagine how frantic Pickford and Addie West must have been a century ago, having only each other to lean on in Wyoming blizzards. They didn't have the luxuries she enjoyed—backup generators, pantries and freezers full of food, and cell phones.

As the fireplace roared and the Christmas tree blinked with brightly colored lights, Kat went down the list of family members to check on.

Gunnar was at the ranch offices with Rowdy and Ash. They had a full plate, taking care of the horses, livestock, and outbuildings. Once everything was secure, they would leave a skeleton crew in charge and come home.

Sassy had arrived safely, thankfully, and was playing with Willow.

Colton and Liu were at the hospital, getting ready to welcome their first child. Kat knew the attending physicians in the West Gorge birthing center, and had great confidence they were in the best hands.

What do people name their Christmas babies? Kat stopped to wonder. Holly, Ivy or Noel? Rudolph, Mary or Joseph? She could hardly wait to hold the little newborn girl or boy—Liu had kept the baby's sex a closely guarded secret!

Ridge and Casey were in one of the barns, uncovering the old family sleigh for the arrival of Santa Claus the next day. The West family children, snug in their cozy pajamas and slippers, loved to listen for the sleigh bells on Christmas Eve each year.

That just left Pike and Paislee, and Daisy—the bride! How the family would manage to get through the blizzard to the wedding venue in town, Kat did not know. The plan was to have a mid-day ceremony, followed by a Christmas Eve luncheon at the Arts and Culture Center. The event room had been decorated for weeks, and the preacher from the little church would be performing the ceremony, provided he could get there.

Darlene was going to stand up for the bride, and Gray would stand with Rowdy. In spite of Gunnar's comforting words, Kat still felt a wave of anxiety at seeing Darlene at a family wedding. The ghost of girlfriends' past was already ruining the blessed event for Kat.

"Good Lord," she exclaimed out loud. "What if she sets her cap for Gray West?" Shaking thoughts of Darlene Shire from her head, Kat realized this was the least of her worries—there wouldn't be a wedding at all if the snow didn't let up soon.

CHAPTER 29

"There you are, I've been trying to reach you, Daisy."

Kat put the phone on speaker, and set it on the kitchen counter while making yet another pot of coffee. With a wedding the next day and Colton and Liu's baby on the way, there was no time to sleep, she figured. It was nearly eleven at night—Gunnar sent her a text saying he was wrapping up at the ranch and would be home soon.

Sassy sat at the kitchen table in flannel pajamas waiting, no doubt, for Ash. Ridge and Casey had gone to bed. Colton sent a message that things were progressing slowly at the hospital.

"Oh, hi Kat," Daisy said sleepily, "what's up?"

What's up—is she kidding?

"Well, Daisy," Kat said, "your wedding is fourteen hours away, and there's a blizzard raging outside. I expect all the men in soon, Rowdy included. I'm wondering if you should get in the most dependable SUV you can and come to the ranch. I expect Pike and Paislee here any time—I don't know what's keeping them. But you're the last piece of the family puzzle."

"Um, yeah," Daisy said slowly. "I'm at Rowdy's house, not far from the ranch entrance. I should probably do that."

Kat wondered if Daisy's family was with her, but didn't want to extend the invitation to the entire Shire family—her parents would be welcome, but having Darlene sleeping under her and Gunnar's roof was taking hospitality too far. Still, she should inquire, she knew.

"Daisy, is your family safe in this storm?"

"Yes, they are, Kat. They're not with me but they're safe."

Kat was relieved, and covered the speaker on the phone so Daisy wouldn't hear her exhaling as loud as she did. They must all be at the bungalow in town, or at Daisy's little house. Kat wondered to herself why Daisy wasn't with them, but she'd ask later.

"Daisy, I've got lots of guestrooms, so bring everything and come here—we plowed the ranch road recently, so you should be okay if you leave soon. Call if you get stuck in a drift and I'll send someone to help you. We'll get to the wedding tomorrow... somehow."

"Yeah, about that..." Daisy started to say more, but Kat saw an incoming call from Colton.

"Gotta cut you off, see you in a bit."

"Okay..."

Daisy hung up and looked at her wedding gown, hanging on a door in Rowdy's house. She would grab the dress and shoes, then throw a few essentials in a suitcase. It made sense that Rowdy would stay close to the ranch, and she wanted to be with him—more than ever.

"Rowdy West, you are something else," Daisy said to herself with a smile as she set her short trip in motion. The ranch road had been plowed, but the snow was coming down hard, and high winds blew drifts over everything. She'd better get going.

I'm coming to you, she texted Rowdy quickly, *see you at the ranch.*

Tomorrow was her scheduled wedding day, and she had been eager to walk towards Rowdy, and her future as Mrs. Rowdy West, in a beautiful lace gown. He was a sucker for lace! With a blush, she recalled how his eyes lit up when she arrived at his doorstep to help him add a few paintings to the walls of his new home. She would point out various artists, but he couldn't take his eyes off of her.

The rest, as they say, was history.

A sudden gust brought her back to the moment and she looked at the windows in fear. She'd better get a move on, and reach safety. In the bathroom, she started throwing things into her makeup bag as the lights flickered, threatening to go out altogether.

"Hurry, girl," she told herself, hearing the panic in her voice. If the storm didn't let up soon, there would be no wedding tomorrow in the Arts and Culture Center. The roads would remain unpassable, and none of the vendors would be able to come. If the power went out, it wouldn't matter if the family could or couldn't make it—they'd have to cancel.

But whatever Christmas Eve would bring, Daisy decided, she and Rowdy would be together at the ranch and they would face it as a team. Turning out the last of the lights, Daisy scooped up her bags, the dress, and her warmest coat and hat, and trudged the short distance to her four wheel drive.

"Let's go find your man," she said to herself.

CHAPTER 30

"Talk to me, Colton," Kat said into her phone, "how is Liu?"

"No news yet, Kat," Colton said, "but we're making good progress. I stepped out of the room for a minute, but can't talk long."

"Right. I know Liu is exhausted, so stay close and help keep her spirits up."

"I'm doing my best, but I admit to feeling inadequate at times," he said.

Kat laughed gently and said, "welcome to parenthood, Colton. That sums it up perfectly."

Colton laughed a little with frustration, exhaustion and hope evident in his voice on the other end of the phone.

"Liu is awesome," he said. "I don't know where she's finding this reserve of strength right now, but I am amazed. I know she kind of wants her mother to be with her too, but she told Ling to wait at the condo for the time being."

"She's very focused, Colton," Kat said, "and you are the person she needs at this moment. You two can do this."

Kat thought back to the sweet moment of delivering little Willow, and the joy she and Gunnar shared when they first saw their daughter's face. The bond between the couple was strengthened, and had only grown stronger in the past six years.

Reflexively, Kat placed her hand on her stomach, remembering how privileged she felt, growing a precious child in her womb; the child of her hero and husband, Gunnar West. When she turned, Sassy was eyeing her suspiciously over a mug of hot chocolate.

"Kat," Colton said, "the nurse is calling me back in. I'll call you as soon as I can and let you know what's going on, okay?"

"I'll keep my phone on me. Give Liu my love—*our* love, from everyone in the family."

Kat exhaled and looked at Sassy with an exhausted smile. "It's going to be a long night, little sister. I'm glad you're here."

Sassy smiled at Kat as she wearily plopped down at the table. While talking with Colton, Kat finished making coffee, pulled a large pot of beef and barley soup from the refrigerator and put it on a burner, and placed a hefty loaf of sourdough bread on a cutting board. The men would be starving and cold when they came in, and she could use a little something, too.

"Are you feeling okay, Kat?" Sassy asked her sister. "You were holding your stomach and looked pale just now. Your hands were shaking when you put the soup on."

"Hmm, good observations," Kat said. "Maybe you should come work with me at the hospital."

"Are you avoiding the actual question?" Sassy asked.

"Sassy, I'm exhausted. This is way past my bedtime and I'm expecting a houseful of cold, hungry family. It's nearly Christmas Eve, and there's Santa… then a wedding… and a snowstorm. And I'm a little hungry."

Kat's voice sounded fragile and a few tears rolled down her cheek, even as she laughed at herself for breaking down.

Sassy reached over and covered Kat's hand, giving it a squeeze. She'd never known her big sister to be anything but capable—it was refreshing to see her human side.

"You can't do anything about the snowstorm, but I don't think you need to worry about Santa. I'm sure he's got everything under control," Sassy said with a smile, getting up to stir the soup and put a ladle-full in a mug for Kat, "and I can take care of your hunger. The wedding though..."

"Poor Daisy and Rowdy. They've been so eager to be married, and Daisy's parents have one foot out of West Gorge already—they're anxious to get out of town and down to warm, sunny weather. If the wedding gets postponed, they could be snowed in. Or worse, they could miss the wedding altogether."

"Let's not borrow trouble," Sassy said, optimistically. "This storm could very well let up any time, giving the snow plows a chance to clear the roads. If the power doesn't go out at the culture center, it could all go as planned tomorrow."

Kat wiped away a tear and sipped a spoonful of the warm soup. This was Sassy's first Wyoming winter and the girl had no idea how the snow could pile up. Unlike gentle Midwest snowstorms, the snow could fall for days in Wyoming, without ceasing. But she liked Sassy's sunny outlook.

"You're right, Sassy," Kat said after biting a spoonful of perfectly seasoned soup, "it's still early enough to get good news."

CHAPTER 31

"I have terrible news!"

Paislee came into the ranch house with a theatrical whisper, and suitcases in each hand. Pike audibly *shushed* the women as he carried a sleeping Sun and Ford, one in each arm. He silently made his way to his childhood suite, where Kat had long ago added a wall of trundle beds for the children. The flannel quilts were already folded down and ready.

After Pike and the kids were out of earshot, Paislee took her coat off and shared her news with Kat and Sassy.

"The officiant cancelled—said he didn't think he'd be able to make it to the wedding in this storm," she said. "The florist said the same and dropped off the flowers in the snow. I managed to save Daisy's bouquet, but the rest froze. The power went out at the center and we don't have backup generators, so no lights or heat."

As the women spoke, Pike went back to his car and began carrying in heavy cardboard boxes, setting them carefully on the kitchen island.

"What's all this?" Kat asked Paislee.

"Fifty beef dinners," was the answer.

"Forty *nine* beef dinners," Pike interjected on his way out, "and one zucchini casserole."

"We already paid the caterer," Paislee said, "so she gave us everything early. She said she couldn't risk getting snowed in at the wedding and missing Christmas with her kids."

"Well at least we know what we're having for Christmas Eve dinner," Kat said.

"And Christmas day," Sassy chimed in. "Now, if only we had dessert."

"I've got the wedding cake in the car," Pike said, trudging through the kitchen again.

The three women looked at each other and laughed, then hugged.

"Merry Christmas," they all said, just as the downstairs door opened and the men began filing in. Kat went and stirred the soup, knowing they would all be hitting the hot showers and changing into the warmest clothes they could after being out in the elements.

Sassy went into the great room and threw a few more logs on the massive fire, and sat down to watch the flames. The last time she'd been in this very spot, Ash had slipped behind her and wrapped his arms around her, then kissed her silly.

The memory made her shudder with pleasure—same with Ash's kiss in the church after Freda's wedding, and in the hallway of the inn they stayed at in Lander.

Things had been steadily heating up between the two of them, until Ash found her job application for the position in Chicago. To his credit, he didn't storm out or jump to conclusions. He merely stayed away, and put some distance between them.

Sassy didn't know what was worse.

But in fairness to Ash, she was allowing him to process changes in plans that weren't his own. In fairness to both of them, they really had no plans as a couple. Only a growing sense of attraction and an increasingly difficult time breaking away from each other. At times, their kisses were too hot to handle—leading Sassy to desire more of Ash than she'd ever wanted from a man before, and more than she'd wanted to give.

It frightened her just a little, or would have if it weren't the honorable Ash West. Though he was struggling too, she could tell.

They needed to either move forward or break off altogether, because keeping their relationship the same wouldn't be possible for much longer.

Nervously, Sassy listened for Ash's voice in the kitchen. They hadn't spoken much since he came to see her in town, only a few cursory texts. And if he wanted to end their relationship it would gut her, but she would keep it together for the sake of Kat, and Christmas.

"Hey." Sassy jumped at the sound of Ash's voice. He sat down close to her on the sofa, and put his arm around her shoulders, pulling her close. *Good sign,* she thought.

"Hey yourself," she turned to face Ash. "I was listening for you, but I guess I didn't do a very good job of it."

Leaning over, Sassy kissed him on his cheek. He smelled like soap, and his hair was still wet from the shower. She didn't know why, but the effect made her want to be close to him—very close. After kissing his cheek, she caught his eyes and brought her mouth to his own lips.

Ash didn't resist; their kiss was long and soft and Sassy felt it down to her toes.

"Wow," he whispered when she pulled away. "I didn't think I'd ever warm up, but that about did it."

Looking in his eyes, Sassy thought she saw sadness there and it just about broke her heart. Was he going to break up with her? She didn't know if she could bear it, even though it might be for the best in the long run.

Maybe their worlds were just too different, and far apart. Although, where in the world would she ever find a man like Ash West—someone so tender hearted?

"I… I should turn in," Sassy said. "Tomorrow's going to be a long day, and Kat's going to need my help."

Ash nodded and smiled weakly. Just then, a clock chimed from the next room, signaling midnight.

"Merry Christmas Eve, Sassy." Ash ran his warm hand up Sassy's arm to her shoulder and then her neck, and ran his fingers through her hair. She closed her eyes at the intimate sensation and exhaled.

"Merry Christmas Eve, Ash," Sassy said back to him, dropping her chin onto her chest. She didn't want him to see the tears she felt pooling in her eyes. As she moved away from him to stand, he caught her elbow and beckoned her to stay.

"Hey," he said, "can we talk for a minute, before you go? I have something to say."

Oh gosh, here it comes, Sassy thought, but stayed still.

"About your job application, in Chicago." Ash continued, "It took me by surprise because I assumed it would be the end of us. But we don't have to end, Sassy. I don't want us to."

"You don't?" Sassy could hear the surprise in her own voice.

"No, I thought you knew that. I told you at Freda's wedding that I love you, and that means we can work anything out," he said. "Tomorrow let's talk more, okay? And... I'm really sorry if my reaction was anything less than excited for you."

CHAPTER 32

"Did Santa come?"

Little Ford West toddled into the big kitchen of the ranch house, where his bleary-eyed parents were drinking coffee along with most of the family. In spite of the howling wind, the ranch house was cozy and warm, with sweet and savory aromas filling the air as breakfast sizzled on the stove.

"Not yet, big guy. He comes tonight, remember?" Pike lifted his sleepy son, who rested his fair head on his dad's shoulder and closed his eyes again. Ridge ruffled Ford's hair as he walked past the pair on the way to the coffee pot to fill his mug.

"Anyone want a refill?"

The chorus of "aye's" were many, including Casey, Kat, Gunnar, Paislee, Sassy and Ash. Sassy gestured for everyone to stay put, while she got up to make more coffee for the crowd. Ash eyed her appreciatively as she crossed the room.

Colton sent Kat a text an hour before, telling her to expect a video chat very soon—everyone was on pins and needles waiting for good news.

By the stove, Casey manned a griddle filled with link sausages. Next to her, Paislee flipped pancakes and stacked them on a warming platter. Gunnar went through the motions of setting plates on the table, along with maple syrup and forks. Ridge filled small glasses with orange, pulpy juice for everyone.

It didn't take more than a glance out the window to see that the snow had only picked up during the night, along with the winds. Everyone shook their head, knowing there would be no formal wedding that afternoon for Rowdy and Daisy. The Arts and Culture Center would be unreachable, and with the power out, there was no use even trying.

"She must be heartbroken," Kat spoke in low tones to the family. "I heard her come in late last night, but she must not have felt like socializing. Rowdy got her settled into a room downstairs, I guess. I just feel so bad for her."

The family murmured and nodded in agreement. Nobody was looking forward to delivering the bad news to Daisy that the wedding had been cancelled, though surely, she could deduce that on her own in seconds.

"Brides are the ultimate optimists," Paislee said to the room.

Just then, Kat's phone started ringing, and she shushed everyone with her hands while wildly gesturing. "It's Colton!"

"Kat," Colton said, "I'm going to call you back in five minutes through video chat, so get everyone together."

Everyone screamed and laughed as they ran into the great room—the big television screen over the fireplace was ready for the call. Casey turned off the stove burners, and Paislee gathered all three kids. Everyone landed hard on the sofas and the floor, all stacked up and bunched together for Colton and Liu to see. When the phone rang again, the group squealed with delight.

"Hey there! Merry Christmas Eve," Colton was grinning broadly as he spoke.

They could see him as he greeted the family, holding a wrapped flannel blanket, which could only contain a baby—just hours old. Everyone hushed and held their breath.

"I'd like you all to meet our little daughter, Jade West. Born just after two this morning."

He folded the edge of the blanket down to show a perfect pink newborn girl, trying to put her fist in her mouth. Her eyes were closed, revealing Jade's long, dark eyelashes, which rested on round porcelain cheeks.

The Wests gasped and sighed and cried out in pure joy at the sight. All but one.

"Aw, shoot. I wanted a *boy* cousin, Uncle Colton," Ford exclaimed.

"Did you?" Colton laughed, as did everyone else. "Well then… everyone… meet Jade's brother, Jackson West."

The earlier gasps had nothing on the hoots and hollers at the revelation that Colton and Liu had birthed twins, on Christmas Eve. Colton turned the camera on his phone to show a bedraggled but glowing Liu, who held a newborn baby identical to Jade in her arms.

"Meet Jade and Jackson," Liu said wearily. "They are our *dragon-phoenix* babies. In Chinese culture, twins bring many blessings, and great good fortune."

"You must have known, Liu," Kat cried out with tears in her eyes, and a radiant smile.

"We did know," Liu confessed, sheepishly, "but kept it a secret from everyone, even my own family. It just seemed too good to be true. I didn't believe it until I had both babies in my arms."

Another secret revealed, Kat thought. Pike and Paislee withheld that they were moving to Denver, and Liu and Colton kept the arrival of the twins to themselves.

Was that all?

Kat knew for a fact that wasn't all, and thought Ridge had been looking a little shifty lately—and Casey was downright guilty of something. But just like newborn twins, everything would be revealed in due time.

After a few more glimpses of the babies, and assurances that mama was doing well, the family reluctantly said goodbye to Colton, Liu, Jackson and Jade West. There were grins and tears aplenty in the room as everyone marveled at the little ones—*two* new babies on the ranch.

"Imagine that." Kat rested her head on Gunnar as he squeezed her tight.

Paislee's smile turned to tears as she buried her face in Pike's flannel shirt. "We're going to miss so much," she cried softly.

"Goodbyes are always hard," he soothed, "but we'll be back in a few months for spring break, and I dare anyone to take those little ones from our arms."

Casey kissed Ridge on the cheek, then got up to check on the state of their Christmas Eve breakfast, calling out to the crowd as she left.

"Cold pancakes anyone?"

CHAPTER 33

After the kids had run off to play with Willow's toys, the rest of the West family lingered in the oversized kitchen in their flannel pajama pants and fleece sweaters, or soft plaid shirts. Everyone took turns stoking the great room fire, brewing more coffee, and washing the dishes.

Christmas music played gently in the background as the snow swirled outside and the wind howled. Everyone was thankful for the emergency generators that took the stress and worry out of the storm. The group had food and coffee for days—and each other.

Board games were brought up from the storage closet, and a box full of stockings to hang on the lodgepole pine mantle.

"Thirteen stockings this year," Kat exclaimed to Paislee. "That's a record. But I have more. Enough for Colton, Liu, and all the Chens, if they were here."

She had a stocking for Gray West, too; he would be spending Christmas in Oregon with fellow wildfire fighters, in light of the snowstorm that grounded him there a few days earlier. And while she didn't mention it, Kat had Christmas stockings for Daisy's parents, in the event they stayed a night after the wedding and joined the family for Christmas morning.

But the stocking she would never hang on her mantle was one for Darlene Shire.

Gazing at the storm, Kat gave quiet thanks that the good Lord had allowed her to avoid the woman for yet another year, even though she'd steeled her heart for the inevitable run-in at Daisy and Rowdy's wedding. While she wouldn't have wished the cancellation for the world, Kat enjoyed the feeling of relief as it washed over her.

She must try not to appear too happy when Daisy came upstairs to join the group, Kat decided, so the disappointed bride didn't take her smile the wrong way. From the sounds of footsteps on the lower level, she wouldn't have to wait long.

The loud chatter hushed as Rowdy walked into the kitchen with Daisy on his arm. Unlike the rest of the family, still dressed for warmth, comfort, and afternoon naps, the two had showered and were wearing jeans and wool sweaters. And far from grieving the turn of events, Daisy appeared to be smiling, peaceful, and downright glowing.

"Good morning, everyone," she beamed. "Merry Christmas Eve!"

The Wests murmured their warm, sympathetic greetings, as a gust of wind against the window reminded everyone what would *not* be taking place that afternoon—Daisy's much anticipated wedding.

"Here, sit down Daisy, Rowdy," Casey jumped up and gestured to two chairs. "We saved breakfast for you, and there's plenty of fresh coffee with all flavors of cream—I have peppermint, or mocha maybe?"

Daisy smiled and sat, while Rowdy blushed and went to pour coffee for he and Daisy.

"I'll get the coffee," he said, giving Casey a hug and kiss on her cheek. "Breakfast smells amazing. I'll take a big stack of whatever you cooked up."

"That a 'boy," said Ridge, giving Rowdy a hard clap on the back. "Every groom needs his strength."

Eyes rolled as just about everyone groaned inwardly at Ridge's comment. Surely, everyone else was thinking the same thing—don't bring up the wedding that cannot be. Apparently, Ridge thought it should be confronted head-on.

"We're all walking on eggshells around you two, because we know how unhappy you must be about the snow storm," Ridge said. "But we'll all roll with the hiccup, right?"

"It's a little more than a hiccup, Dad," Gunnar offered. "But Ridge is right. We're all just really sorry that you two can't have your fancy wedding this afternoon, as planned."

"We *are* sorry," Paislee gushed to her friend, "and we understand if your heart is broken over the cancellation, Daisy."

"You have every right to be sad at not being married today," Kat offered.

Daisy stood up and walked over to Rowdy, who wrapped his arms around her in a tight bear hug. She buried her face in his sweater, then looked up at him with a smile. Turning to the family, Daisy inhaled nervously and spoke.

"Yeah… about that."

CHAPTER 34

"You did *what?*"

"Say that again?"

The Wests were incredulous at Daisy's words, and sure they didn't hear her right the first time. As *Jingle Bells* played happily through speakers, Daisy repeated herself.

"It's true—Rowdy and I are already married," she said. "Two days ago, we went to the courthouse to pick up our license with my parents and my sister."

"The office was going to close early because of the storm," Rowdy added.

"My parents were anxious, I knew. As much as they wanted to stay for my wedding, they really wanted to hit the road before the storm stranded them for another week. The moving van would be arriving in Florida, and they needed to be there. And flights were about to get cancelled."

"Darlene was getting antsy about the weather," Rowdy interjected. "She didn't want to stay in West Gorge any longer than she had to."

"So… we got married at the courthouse then and there, with my family as witnesses. I've officially been Daisy West for two days…"

"…and two nights," Rowdy whispered under his breath. Daisy

grinned broadly, and held up her hand to show the wedding band that accompanied her beautiful engagement ring. Rowdy lifted his hand too, then kissed his wife on the lips.

After a moment of stunned silence, Gunnar yelled out a loud *whoop,* and the rest of the family followed. Rowdy and Daisy opened their arms to hugs and kisses, smiles and tears. Shouts of *Congratulations!* filled the air, as the kitchen gathering became a party.

"You ol' dog," Gunnar said to Rowdy. "No wonder you've been in a daze on the ranch."

When the excitement quieted down, Daisy explained that her mother and father left right after the courthouse ceremony and drove safely to Colorado, south of the storm. They dropped Darlene off at the Denver airport, and were now almost to their new home in Florida.

"I'm gonna miss your dad. Sorry I didn't get to say a proper goodbye," Ridge said, "maybe Casey and I will make it down there for a visit—especially now that we're family."

Daisy hugged Ridge, and said how much his friendship meant to Bud Shire over the years. "He will miss you too, Ridge. I know for a fact he will."

Ridge nodded and blinked away a tear.

"I'm going to miss his house, too," he said with a small laugh. "I'm trying to forgive him, though. But I sure did picture myself sitting on that front porch in my old age, and watching the town go by."

Daisy hugged him again, then went to find her husband.

As the excitement quieted down, Paislee spoke up to the room.

"Hey, we may have missed the wedding," she said, "but we've got the food, the cake and the bouquet. Daisy, you've got the pretty dress and the handsome groom."

Kat brightened. "What do you say, Daisy, how about a Christmas Eve wedding party on the ranch?"

CHAPTER 35

As the excitement of a wedding reception gripped the family, Casey pulled Ridge into the great room to sit by the fire with her.

"That's right," he said, "we'll let those kids figure out the details and tell us where we need to be, and when."

"Maybe you can get away with that, but I'll be glad to pitch in. I just thought we could sit and enjoy the Christmas tree and the fire for a few minutes and catch our breath—what a busy morning this has been."

Ridge shook his head in wonder.

"*Two* new grandbabies. I can scarcely believe it. Jackson and Jade West."

"Such cute babies," Casey agreed. "They'll be home in just days. As soon as the storm stops long enough to plow the main roads, right?"

"That's right." Ridge squeezed Casey tight, remembering the storm that was raging when he ventured up to the pass to rescue his love from the elements and the wild animals. He hadn't fully known until that day how much he loved Casey, or the fact that he was rescuing his soon-to-be wife. Now, he was the happiest of men.

"Hey, Ridge," Casey moved away from him slightly. "I have an early Christmas present for you. I think now is a good time."

"For me? I thought we weren't giving each other presents this year."

Ridge and Casey West had every earthly thing they could ever want, and only wanted to travel and see the world together, in between spending precious time with family and friends. Of course, he put a beautiful diamond bracelet under the Christmas tree for his bride, but never expected a gift in return.

Casey padded over to the tree and made of show of looking at all the gifts underneath—there must have been a hundred or so wrapped presents. But then she looked at Ridge with a twinkle in her eye and reached up for a small box that was sitting on a branch.

"I do think this is it," she said, mischievously.

"But that's so small," Ridge teased. "How can that be my Harley Davidson?"

"Not on my watch, buddy," Casey teased back. "They say that good things come in small packages, so let's see what's in here."

Sitting next to Ridge again, Casey leaned in for a full kiss on his warm handsome mouth. She placed a free hand on his face and caressed the soft stubble that she found so appealing in its ruggedness.

"Mmm, you taste like maple syrup," he whispered with a smile.

"Open the present," she pulled away and said, "I can't wait a minute longer."

Ridge raised his eyebrows with interest and looked at the little box —small, but expertly wrapped in gold paper. He pulled on the red ribbon and the box easily fell off. Then, he pulled at a taped corner until the paper was gone, and he was holding an unmarked wooden box with a brass hinge on one side.

"What's in here?" Ridge opened the box to reveal a set of keys, held together with a simple gold circle. "Hmm. Now tell me, Casey girl, I've already unlocked your heart, so what do these keys open?"

With a sigh and a smile, Casey gazed at Ridge and floored him with her words.

"They open the front door of a certain Craftsman bungalow in downtown West Gorge, a bungalow that is now yours. Ours. Front porch and all."

As Ridge's mouth gaped in surprise, Casey went on to tell him that after selling all her properties in town, she hired a law firm to approach the Shires with an offer they couldn't turn down.

"Bud and his wife truly had no idea it was me buying their house, for you. The lawyer told them his client would work with any timeframe that suited them, and offered far too much money."

Casey went on to suggest that she and Ridge could now divide their time between Phoenix and West Gorge, Wyoming, settling into the little town house for the summer. They hadn't yet told the family that they'd also be leaving after Christmas, and unlike previous years, they wouldn't be back in town for several months.

"That front porch... is ours?" Ridge was still amazed. "With all the things I've owned during my life, that house, and that front porch, has been calling me for as long as I can remember. I didn't think I could be any happier today, but this is remarkable, Casey."

Casey couldn't smile any broader—as it was, she felt so much happiness at giving this special gift to her husband. There wasn't much you could give the man who really did have everything, but she'd managed to do just that.

"While we're away this winter, we can have a few things done in the house. Amber said she'd oversee any projects, and the delivery of new furniture and such. When we come home in the spring, everything will be perfect and waiting for us," Casey told Ridge.

"You're just perfect," Ridge said, taking her hands in his own. "Thank you for this."

CHAPTER 36

"Thought I might find you here."

Ash wandered into a den off the great room. By contrast, it was smaller than the other rooms in the rambling ranch house, but large enough for a family-size sectional sofa, a more manageable gas fireplace, and built-in bookcases. On a television screen, *A Wonderful Life* played on mute, while Sassy was curled up on the sofa, watching.

Kat had a trim pine tree brought into the den, and the twinkling white lights showed off an array of hand-blown glass ornaments of birds, pinecones, and log cabins. The affect was rustic and charming, and perfect for the space. The warmth of the fire and the lights brought out the fresh scent of the tree, filling the air with a pine-forest aroma.

Outside, the wind blew snow past the window and onto trees and rocks. In the distance, a small sliver of the gorge was still visible through the storm. Sassy patted the space next to where she sat, inviting Ash to sit down and share the wool blanket that covered her legs.

Ash carefully handed her a mug of hot cocoa, and held his own as he joined her.

"I'm learning a bit about you, Sassy Tate," he said, taking a sip from his mug.

"Oh?"

"You prefer cozy nooks and smaller crowds."

"Thirteen people is hardly a crowd," she answered quietly, taking a sip of the warm drink.

Ash laughed.

"It's a crowd when most everyone is a West—that's a loud bunch," he said.

Sassy regarded him and raised her mug in acknowledgment.

"I'm learning a few things about you too, Ash West," she said, slyly.

"Oh?"

"Yes. You are generous and giving to those you love," she said. "And you find great comfort in being amongst those loud and boisterous Wests out there."

Ash frowned. "Is that a bad thing?"

"No," Sassy was quick to say. "That's a good thing. I can see that you draw strength from the West men—from Ridge, Gunnar, Pike and Rowdy. Colton, too. They really love you, and go out of their way to keep you in their sights. The women do as well. It's a great family you have, Ash."

"It's a start," he replied with a grin, placing his warm hand on Sassy's leg.

"I'm serious, Ash." Sassy sat up straight and looked him in the eye. "This is where you should be. I'm convinced that West Gorge, Wyoming, is where you are going to be the best and strongest version of yourself. This ranch—these people—it's a gift that you shouldn't turn your back on."

"You mean, I shouldn't come with you to Chicago." As Ash spoke, Sassy could see a dark cloud cross his face. She swallowed hard and chose her words carefully.

"For one thing, I haven't been offered a job in Chicago. Yet, anyway. For another thing, there's a lot you don't know about that position."

"I know it's not in Wyoming," he said. "What else is there to know?"

Ash pulled his hand away from her leg and turned towards the fire. As he drank from his mug, Sassy knew he was wrestling with the impulse to flee from her, and from the pain she was trying hard not to inflict on him.

They were both young and growing up fast, thanks to the feelings they shared and the potential conflicts they faced. Their first love was burning hot, but that meant the pain they could cause the other would be just as hot. That wasn't Sassy's intent, and she didn't think it was Ash's either.

"You're jumping to conclusions," Sassy stated. "That hasn't served us well, Ash. I think it's time you and I put all our cards on the table, and see where we both stand."

Ash turned his head towards Sassy. His eyes sparked with the reflection from the fire, and his eyebrows were knitting with an intensity she'd seen only rarely as he gazed at her.

"If I put all my cards on the table, I'm afraid you're going to sweep them onto the floor with your pretty arm, Sass," he said.

Sassy watched him for a few moments, then stood up, leaning down and softly kissing his lips. She held the position for a long while, but he only thawed and returned the kiss as she was about to pull away.

He's hurting, she knew.

"That's a risk I think you should take, Ash."

CHAPTER 37

"Is this silly, do you think?"

Daisy and Rowdy walked into the guestroom at the ranch they had shared the night before, to get ready for their makeshift wedding reception. They were staying in a well-appointed suite on the lower level of the ranch, far away from the family spaces on the main floor. Everyone assumed the two had stayed in separate quarters, but then, it hadn't been revealed that they were already wed.

"Is *what* silly?" Rowdy gently but firmly stopped his wife in her tracks and pulled her close to his chest, wrapping his arms around her with great happiness.

"Staging a pretend wedding ceremony when we're already married?"

Rowdy watched the uncertainty on her face appear like a shadow, and instinctively leaned down to kiss her softly on her cheek.

"There's nothing silly or pretend about it—this is our day to celebrate, Mrs. West. And there's nothing pretend about receiving a family blessing, or the memories we are about to make. To be honest," he continued, "I'm glad to have the pre-wedding jitters behind me, and to actually be your husband. No regrets."

"No regrets for me either," she said. "It all worked out quite well, when you think of it. My family got to be with me for the most important part, and your family is with us for the fun part."

Though they knew both Kat and Darlene were anxious about being in the same room for the wedding, there was no way around it, and Daisy and Rowdy were determined not to let it ruin their big day. As it turned out, the weather wreaking havoc spoiled some things, but solved other things.

"Put on that lace dress I've been dreaming about, and let's enjoy our wedding."

She smiled up at her new husband, and felt a flood of love for the man.

"But what are you going to wear?" Daisy asked. "Jeans and flannel?"

Rowdy looked thoughtful. "I tried to get away with that, but Kat shut me down; said Pike would be taking pictures for the family wall, and told me I'd better go shopping in Gunnar's closet. So that's what I'm going to do while you're getting all pretty."

He smiled and kissed her again, this time it was a slow but insistent kiss on her lips.

"You'd better get going," Daisy said with a sultry laugh, "or we'll get back to the honeymoon and miss our wedding altogether."

As he kissed her again, a knock on the door interrupted them.

"Break it up, you two," Paislee shouted, good-naturedly, "it's time for the bride to have her hair and makeup done."

"Ah well, that's my cue to go find the boys," Rowdy said to Daisy. He opened the door to find Paislee holding a basket of hair curlers, brushes and makeup. Behind her stood Willow and Sun, wearing long plaid dresses with black velvet bows in their hair.

"My helpers are with me," Paislee explained, moving into the room.

"Uncle Rowdy, my daddy says the men are waiting for you upstairs," Willow said.

"Uh oh, then I'd better get a move on," he said with a laugh and a slight bow.

Minutes later, Rowdy walked into Gunnar's suite where the men were waiting for him—all except Ash, who was helping Sassy set the formal dining room for the wedding supper they would all share later.

The house was slowly filling with savory aromas from the catered dinners, warming in the kitchen's double ovens. On one end of the large island sat the two tiered wedding cake, flanked by china plates and sterling forks. On the other end, a wooded salad bowl was filled with field greens and heirloom tomatoes, waiting to be tossed with dressing.

The great room, he could see, had been cleared of the kids' toys, and set up for a ceremony in front of the massive stone fireplace. The snow swirling against the tall picture windows looked to Rowdy like wedding lace in the dim light of the stormy sky.

Everywhere he looked, candles were burning and lights twinkled.

The West women, in flannel pajamas just an hour ago, were beginning to appear throughout the house in shimmery gowns, with hair piled on their heads, held back with crystal pins. The men, he'd soon find out, were dressed in "Western formal" attire, which meant pressed jeans, tucked-in collared shirts, and sport coats. The boots were on, but the cowboy hats stayed on pegs for the time being.

Quietly, by the large Christmas tree, little Ford played with a truck. Like the girls, he was dressed for the event. His fair hair still held a shine from the wet comb that tried to tame it.

Yippee ki yay, it's my wedding day, Rowdy thought with a whistle and a relaxed grin.

CHAPTER 38

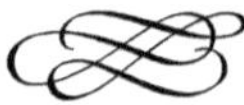

"Take your pick, cousin," Gunnar said, taking Rowdy into his walk-in closet. "Shirts and ties, sport coats, jeans and belts… I reckon you'll want your own boots."

"That's right," Rowdy said, "but you've got a nice collection."

Ridge walked in just then, with Pike close behind. The men had shaved their Christmas Eve stubble and looked ready for a night out—which would be a night in, thanks to the weather.

"Don't forget a little cologne," Pike said, "I have a very reliable source that tells me the ladies love it."

Ridge whistled in agreement. "That they do," Ridge said. And then to Rowdy, "I suppose there's no point asking if you have cold feet, and want us to find you a chicken exit."

"Nope, that ship has sailed," Rowdy said with a grin. He closed the closet door on the men, slightly, and slipped on a white linen shirt. After buttoning it, he tucked it smoothly into a pair of pressed but faded jeans, and opened the door again.

"Tie or no tie?"

"No tie," the West men said in unison, and laughed.

"Once she gets you in a necktie, it's all over," Ridge said.

"But I thought they were for weddings and funerals," Rowdy wondered.

"Just funerals, nephew," Ridge said emphatically.

Gunnar guided the groom to his rack of wool blazers and took three off the hangers for his cousin to try on. They all settled on a charcoal gray, with a cranberry pocket square for the holiday.

"I cleaned your boots for you," Ash said, walking into the room.

The men admired the youngest West, who looked dapper in his dress duds.

"Thank you, thank you very much," Ash responded with a smile, doing his best Elvis Pressley imitation. "Kat insists I keep my closet ready for anything."

"Mine too," Gunnar said with appreciation in his voice.

"Rowdy, you and I were the only single guys left in the family," Ash said, "but now you've gone and left me all alone."

"Maybe not for long," Pike said from a chair in the corner, "from the way I see you looking at Sassy, that is."

Ash blushed, but nodded.

"I wish it were that easy," Ash said.

"It's never easy," Pike replied, "but always worth it."

In Daisy's room, the women were finished getting the bride get ready and declared her to be stunning. She wore an ivory lace dress and red satin shoes. Dangling from her ears were diamond snowflake earrings; a wedding gift from her parents. Daisy's wavy hair hung loose, with a few curls held back.

"You look like a princess," Sun said, adoringly.

Paislee wiped away a tear, and hugged her friend gently.

"I can hardly believe that my good friend is now part of the West family," Paislee said. "I couldn't be happier for you, or for Rowdy."

The rest of the women agreed and in turn, welcomed her into the clan with a kiss on her flushed cheeks. At last, a small messenger came into the room, bearing news for all.

"Let's do this," said tiny Ford West. "I'm starving."

CHAPTER 39

Once upon a time, the great room of the West Ranch had seemed oversized and cavernous to Ridge. When Randi Lynn contracted the construction and design of the home, a young Ridge balked at the massive size.

"This room is bigger than the barn," he protested.

Randi Lynn, hearing the echoes of their two children as they ran around on the plywood floors of the framed house, rubbed her growing belly, and allowed Ridge to run out of steam before smiling peacefully.

"You'll see," she said. "It's big now, but someday this room won't be big enough. It will be wall to wall Wests, and you'll wished we'd gone a little bigger."

"Bah," Ridge spat, but quickly apologized to his young wife. She'd walked away from the life she knew—the life her own parents had laid out for her—to take on the wild and wooly Wyoming ranch, and the man who ran it. Randi Lynn never second guessed his decisions when it came to the ranch, and he tried hard to step back and let her lead when it came to her domains.

And the big family ranch home was definitely his bride's domain.

She had a vision for everything he bristled against and now took for granted. The mudroom and showers in the lower level that allowed the cowboys to join the family looking and smelling like civilized men; the massive kitchen and island that drew everyone together after a long day; even the suites and guestrooms that Ridge once thought were "overkill."

Randi Lynn blessed local artists and artisans by incorporating their antler chandeliers, live-edge wood tables, pearl-inlay clocks, and stone masonry into the home. The fireplace alone soared two stories or higher, and was flanked by windows that captured the breathtaking gorge and mountains the Wests had always been honored to have as their view.

The same gorge his great grandfather, Pickford West, had captured on canvas after arriving on a covered wagon so many years before.

On this Christmas, as Ridge took his place by the stone fireplace, Randi Lynn's words from long ago came flooding back to him.

You'll see; someday this room won't be big enough.

A lump in Ridge's throat was hard to swallow as he felt her presence—she'd been right, of course. He only wished Randi Lynn could be with them today to see how her family had grown. Wouldn't she just love to see the perfect round faces of Colton's newborn babies this morning, all wrapped up and warm in their mom and dad's arms?

Ridge shook his head with wonder. Colton was a daddy. The loveable pup of a boy had become a man with the help of the lovely Liu Chen, and was now the father of twins. Next Christmas, they'd be toddling around the room, holding on to tables and pulling ornaments off the big tree.

A tear escaped the rancher's eye and made its way down his lined cheek, as Casey gave him a look from across the room. He winked at her, letting her know he was okay, and then blew her a kiss. How blessed could a man be, to have two great loves in one lifetime.

Holding the family bible in his hands, Ridge watched as one by one, the West family entered the room and found their place.

Kat, in a cranberry velvet gown, held Gunnar's arm as they walked to the center of the room and sat on the leather sofa. "Fitting," Ridge thought; they were the center of the family. Willow ran into the room and snuggled in next to Kat.

Pike and Paislee walked in together next. She wore a shimmery silver dress with sparkling ruby earrings. Pike held Ford in his arms, who rested his head sleepily on his daddy's shoulder. They settled on another sofa, and pulled Sun between them.

Casey, in her own unpresuming manner, settled off to the side in a wing chair. She wore a beautiful black velvet gown with the pearl earrings and necklace he'd given her this Christmas—a poor second to the gift she'd given him, the Craftsman house in downtown West Gorge. Casey's thoughtfulness knew no bounds, he realized, vowing to up his game in the coming year.

The next couple took his breath away.

Ash walked into the great room with Sassy on his arm, looking for all the world like two people in love. She sparkled and shimmered and glowed as she stole glances at his youngest son, the boy who was growing up before his eyes. Their love for each other was apparent, if only they could reconcile the differences that seemed to hover between them.

The two held hands and settled into a loveseat.

As the sound system in the room played a string version of *Silent Night,* Rowdy entered the room and made his way to the fireplace. The cold weather and the exertion from his hard work made his limp more pronounced than usual, but the smile on his face was all anyone could see.

When Rowdy turned and stood next to Ridge, the elder shook his hand, then thinking better of it, pulled him into a warm embrace.

All eyes turned as Daisy stepped into the room from the foyer, and locked eyes with her husband. Her bouquet of poinsettias, white roses and evergreens trembled, as did the hands that held it. With candle-light and firelight warming the room, Daisy smiled radiantly and walked slowly towards Rowdy.

Taking her hand in his, the couple turned together to face Ridge as did the family gathered in the room; a room that was "wall to wall Wests." Just like Randi Lynn had predicted so many years before. In another lifetime.

CHAPTER 40

"Our days are numbered," Ridge began quietly, after clearing his throat. "Something an old man doesn't like to think about, and something a young man never thinks about."

There were smiles and light laughter at the comment.

"But standing in front of my entire family, nearly everyone, as the eldest," he said somberly, "it's hitting me harder than I'd like it to. I imagine that everyone who came before me said the same thing—from old Pickford to my own parents. Everyone's in here, in the family bible, including Rowdy's parents. We all think we're going to live forever, but we don't. God Himself tells us our days are numbered and to make each one count."

Ridge lifted the book in his hand slightly.

"This day counts," Ridge continued, "on this day we will add the marriage of Rowdy West and Daisy Shire to the family bible, thus continuing the family legacy."

"Here here," Gunnar said, softly. Kat smiled beside him.

"Rowdy," Ridge said, looking directly at his nephew, "the words in first Corinthians about love could easily be said about you. If Daisy hasn't discovered this by now, let me just say that you're a fine man, and I'm proud to be your uncle. Your parents would be busting their buttons standing here, witnessing your devotion to Daisy."

Daisy squeezed her husband's arm while Rowdy swallowed hard.

"First Corinthians tells us that love is patient and kind, and does not envy or boast. It's not proud; it does not dishonor others. It's not self-seeking or easily angered; it keeps no record of wrongs. Love does not delight in evil but rejoices with the truth. It always protects, always trusts, always hopes and perseveres."

"And Daisy, I don't know you quite as well, yet, but welcome to the family. You have our love and support from the get go."

This time, the chorus of "here here's" was more pronounced as everyone joined in.

Ridge gazed around the room at his loved ones. He had dreaded this when Kat asked him to preside over the makeshift ceremony, but now realized what a privilege it was to be able to speak to everyone. He only wished Colton and Liu could be here, but his heart flooded with joy and warmth at the thought of babies Jackson and Jade.

"Now then," Ridge said, "before I lose the room, and before little Ford dies of hunger, I have a final prayer to read, and I want everyone to listen. This prayer, by a Dr. Louis Evans, has been tucked in the bible for years. My mother used to read it at weddings. As a boy, I thought it would be the death of me, waiting for her to finish so we could eat cake—but what I wouldn't give to hear her sweet voice now," he said.

Ridge cleared his throat again, and a few sniffs were heard in the room.

"Oh God of love, Thou has established marriage for the welfare and happiness of mankind. Thine was the plan, and only with Thee can we work it out with joy. Bless this husband. Bless him as provider of nourishment and raiment, and sustain him in all the exactions and pressures of his battle for bread. May his strength be her protection, his character be her boast and her pride, and may he so live that she will find him the haven for which the heart of woman truly longs."

Ridge looked over at Casey and continued once he caught her eye.

"Bless this loving wife. Give her tenderness that will make her great, a deep sense of understanding, and a great faith in Thee. Give her that inner beauty of soul that never fades, that eternal youth that is found in holding fast the things that never age. Teach them that marriage is not living merely for each other; it is two uniting and joining hands to serve Thee. Give them great spiritual purpose in life. May they seek first the kingdom of God and His righteousness, and the other things shall be added unto them."

The Wests were enraptured by the words, and by Ridge's earnest tone as he finished.

"May they never take each other's love for granted, but always experience that breathless wonder that exclaims: *Out of all this world, you have chosen me.* When life is done and the sun is setting, may they be found then as now, hand in hand, still thanking God for each other. May they serve Thee happily, faithfully, together, until at last, one shall lay the other into the arms of God. This we ask through Jesus Christ, great Lover of our souls."

By the time Ridge folded up the prayer and tucked it once again in the bible, there wasn't a dry eye in the room, except for those of the children, napping in their parents' arms.

"You've already been pronounced husband and wife," Ridge said, smiling, "so I'll just say this last thing—Rowdy, you can kiss your bride."

As everyone stood and cheered, Rowdy took Daisy in his arms and kissed her on the lips. She wrapped her arms around his shoulders and melted into her tall and wonderful cowboy. One by one, each person kissed and hugged the new couple, and made their way into the dining room for dinner.

"I wonder if we're having beef," Rowdy could be heard to say.

CHAPTER 41

After the kids had run off from the table to go and watch out the window for Santa, the ten adults sipped their coffee and enjoyed a slice of wedding cake for dessert. The women had all pitched in, pulling the feast together, and the men would do the same for the cleanup. But on this Christmas Eve, no one was eager to do much except reminisce about the newborn twins, the wedding ceremony, and what would be the last holiday with Pike and Paislee in West Gorge until spring.

"I guess it's time that Casey and I told you all that we're doing the same," Ridge said, getting his family's attention. "We decided to spend our winter in Phoenix; and not just for a few weeks, like in past years."

Collective groans around the table revealed disappointment.

"What are we going to do without you?" Kat pouted, reaching out to squeeze Casey by the hand. The two had become true friends since Ridge married her, and they spent long hours discussing many topics of interest to both women.

"Well, anytime the airport is open, you can fly down to see us, that's what," Casey said. "The Phoenix house has two guestrooms, and we can walk to boutiques and restaurants, and art galleries." Casey looked pointedly at both Daisy and Paislee as well as Kat.

"Ash," Ridge chimed in, "you and Sassy would like the coffee shops in the neighborhood. The area has a good 'vibe,' or so I'm told."

Everyone laughed good-naturedly at the comment.

"I'll miss you, Dad," Ash said. "I'll miss you too, Pike. And you, Paislee. Even the kids. It just won't seem the same with everyone gone."

"Some of us are staying," Gunnar said with a smile. "And I sure hope you're not going anywhere, Ash. Seems like you just came home from Michigan after four long years."

Sassy looked at Ash with interest, wondering, no doubt, what his answer would be.

"Who can say," Ash said with a tease of a grin, reaching under the table for Sassy's hand. "I thought I had everything figured out, but who knows what tomorrow's going to bring."

"It's going to bring lots of toys and candy, Uncle Ash," Ford West declared to the room. The little boy had slipped into his mother's arms and was sharing her cake.

The room let out a laugh and the men took that as a cue to begin clearing the table.

"Don't get up, Rowdy," Pike said to his cousin. "This is your party."

"Oh no. You're not leaving me here with all the women—I'm coming with you." Rowdy stood and gathered Daisy's dishes, then leaned down to give her a soft and lingering kiss. The West women at the table hooted and laughed, tapping the sides of their crystal champagne flutes with the tines of their silver forks.

"Wait, before you go," Daisy told him, motioning for him to come closer as she whispered something in his ear.

"Yes ma'am," he agreed, seductively.

"Are you going to tell us what she's saying?" Ridge, back in the room, whistled.

"The lady wants more coffee," Rowdy deadpanned.

"Honestly, this is the best Christmas Eve I've ever known." Casey wiped a tear from her cheek, while smiling and sniffing at the same time.

"Me too," Daisy said, doing the same. "Thank you all from the bottom of my heart for everything—my wedding could not have worked out more perfectly."

"I'm sorry your parents couldn't stay, Daisy," Kat said.

"I know, but it's okay. I've seen them nearly every day of my life, you know. And this is a new chapter for them, as well as for me. I'm only glad they got out of West Gorge ahead of the storm."

"Speaking of the storm, look," Paislee said, pointing to the window, "the wind has stopped, and only a few snowflakes are falling now."

Everyone turned to see the darkening sky. No longer beating and swirling against the windows, the snow had indeed abated to lovely decorative flakes. Outside, the pines were frosted and white, and the ground had a pillowy covering, like a blanket of feathers.

"Just like a Christmas card," Sassy sighed.

From the kitchen, the women could hear the men laughing, loudly clanging the dishes, and somebody snapping a dish towel.

"Best not to go in there," Kat said with a smile to the other women.

"You'll be lucky to have any china intact after tonight," said Paislee, who had grown up with sisters in a fully staffed household.

"Probably." Kat gazed out the window as she spoke. "When I first came to the ranch, there was so much sadness in this house. A lot of fragile hearts—my own included. The men were all privately nursing their own wounds, not letting each other in. But now, just listen."

As the dining room fell quiet, they heard the men talking and joking with each other, and miraculously, the sounds of plates being hand dried and carefully stacked.

"Wow, it's quiet in here." Ash walked into the dining room with a damp towel over his shoulder and a fresh pot of coffee, which he poured into each woman's cup. "What are we listening to?"

"Family," was the unanimous answer.

CHAPTER 42

The volume of the children's voices had reached a high, fevered pitch as they anticipated the arrival of Santa. Even the warm baths and cozy flannel pajamas couldn't make a dent in their excitement.

"Shh," Kat encouraged, as the three ran around the great room. "If you are quiet and listen, you might hear Santa and his sleigh." Willow, Sun and Ford would stop for a theatrical moment, and then one would squeal, setting off a chain reaction.

"Wait, wait, wait," Willow said to the others, "I think I really do hear him—listen."

"I don't hear anything," Ford protested loudly, causing the girls to yell.

"You can't hear 'cause you're too *loud*," Sun told her brother.

Panting and out of breath, Ford at last quieted down to hear the sound that was coming nearer and nearer—unmistakably, everyone could hear sleigh bells.

As they jumped up and down, Kat guided the children to a front window, where they could see lights on a sleigh heading through the snow towards the house. Pulled by two bedecked and jingling horses, the sleigh easily slid right up to the now open front door, where the children stood in stunned silence.

Three little mouths gaped as the driver, clad in heavy red velvet from head to toe, and a curly snow white beard, said "whoaaaa" to the horses, and stepped down from the sleigh. He waved a leather mitten at the children, then reached into the back seat and pulled out a large red velvet sack, tied with a silk cord.

Turning around towards the door, he placed his hand on his hip and laughed out loud.

"*Ho Ho Ho, Merry Christmas!* Merry Christmas. Is this the home of Willow, Sun and Ford? Or do I have the wrong address?"

Tongue tied and speechless, the children could only nod. When the jolly man began walking towards the door, the three screamed in delight and ran towards the big tree in the great room, where the only lights were from the tree itself, the fireplace, and several flickering candles. In addition to the many flashes from Pike's camera.

"Well, look who's here," Gunnar said enthusiastically as he greeted the guest. "Santa, we weren't certain you were going to make it tonight in this snowstorm. Come on in and sit by the fire. We sure are glad to see you."

"Oh now, Gunnar," Santa said in a deep baritone, "did I ever let you down when you were a boy, or your brothers, Pike, Colton and Ash?"

"No sir," Gunnar answered with a shake of the head. "You've never let me down."

"He knows all our *uncles*," Sun whispered to the others, amazed.

"Yes, I do know your uncles—I know everyone in your family, Sun," Santa Claus said to the room as he sat upon a large chair by the tree. "And everyone has been very, very good this year."

As the children jumped in uncontained joy, Santa motioned for them to sit on the floor so he could unpack his sack.

"Now, wait a minute, where in the world is Jackson and Jade West?"

"They just got born," Ford said.

"Jackson and Jade are in the hospital," Willow informed Santa. "But I don't think they'll let you in. Security is tight."

As the Wests laughed, Santa smiled.

"Then I'll just leave their presents at their house, okay?"

The children looked at each other and nodded their consent.

"Now then," he said, "I'm very busy tonight, so I can't stay long. And I'll be back again later, *after* you go to sleep. But I do have a few things in my bag to give you now."

The three bounced and bobbed happily as their parents smiled and took pictures. The children were so enraptured with the surprise visit and the gifts they were being handed, that they didn't notice the absence of their grandfather, or the quiet disappearance of Ash and Sassy.

With the music playing throughout the house, neither did they hear the bells on the sleigh as it drove away from the house.

CHAPTER 43

"That was awesome," Sassy said to Ash, as they snuggled in the front seat of the sleigh.

"Thanks for coming with me," he said. "I told Dad I'd sneak this away and get the horses back to the barn. It's too cold for them to be out too long.

"Same with me. But for the moment, I'm cozy and warm," she said, tucked under a heavy wool blanket.

"Good, then we can enjoy a little sleigh ride before we go back to the crowd."

"I admit to being a little overwhelmed at times in this group. As you know, it was just me and my mom and dad at Christmas. The day was always fun and magical, but much quieter than a West Christmas on the ranch."

Ash nodded a little sadly and gently flicked the reign to keep the horses moving through the fresh snow. Their hooves made a muffled clomp with each step.

"My Christmases were quiet growing up," he said. "Mainly because my parents never put up a tree, or made a big deal about it. My granny would send money for me, but they usually spent it on themselves before I even knew about it."

"That's just..." Sassy struggled for the words that would convey her heartbreak for Ash.

"No!" Ash smiled over at her and tried to recover. "I don't want to make you sad tonight. I'm just saying that for me, the family Christmas is overwhelming, but in a good way. They've knocked themselves out creating new memories for me, and for everyone. I kind of like the over-the-top stuff."

"Then I do too," Sassy whispered, gazing up at a sky filled with bright stars and breathing the crisp, cold air.

"I also like being with you, out here in the quiet," Ash said tentatively, "and..."

There was silence, except for the bells on the horse's reigns.

"And?" Sassy asked.

She looked over at Ash, who handled the reigns and the sleigh with such confidence, as if he were born and raised on the ranch. Unlike the Ash she first met, who had been riddled with insecurities, he had a peaceful smile on his face, which was pink and ruddy from the cold. As he exhaled, puffs of breath were visible in the night air.

Ash West looked very much a man, she thought, drawn to him in a powerful way.

He looked over at her with a smile she could see in the moonlight, and then guided the sleigh to a clearing where he pulled to a stop. As the horses bobbed their heads, the bells jangled. Otherwise, the only sounds were from a gentle wind high in the pines.

"Snow will be picking up again soon," Ash said, looking at the night sky.

"I guess we better enjoy this while we can," Sassy whispered with a reverence the silent night seemed to call for.

Ash tied the reigns to the front of the sleigh, then turned his body slightly towards her.

"I love you, Sassy."

Smiling, she watched Ash reach into the pocket of his jacket and pull out a small velvet box. She almost made a joke, asking him if he snitched it from Santa's sack, but thankfully, thought better of it.

Be still, a voice inside her cautioned. *Whatever this moment is, it belongs to Ash.*

He was struggling to find words, she could see. At last, he leaned towards her and kissed her gently on the lips.

"I had this all planned out, but my thoughts have left me," he confessed. "They amounted to this: Will you marry me, Sassy, and be my wife?"

As her mouth fell open in surprise, so did the little velvet box, revealing a diamond solitaire sitting on a diamond studded gold band. It sparkled under the light of the moon, and the battery-powered lights that outlined the sleigh.

In her stunned silence, she looked up in shock at Ash, who rushed on with other thoughts as if suddenly remembering them.

"I'll move to Chicago with you, and figure out what I can do there," he said.

"You will?"

"Yeah," he said. "As much as I love the ranch, I want to be with you even more."

She could hardly believe what she was hearing, and said as much. Ash, beginning to get discouraged as he held out the opened box, felt a lump forming in his throat.

"That is almost as monumental as the question you just asked me," Sassy said.

He lowered his head as he looked at her.

"I want you to know that if you say *yes*, you won't be marrying the ranch. Just the man."

A slow smile formed on Sassy's face, and Ash could see a tear run down her cheek, red from the cold winter air. She brought her mittened hands up to her face.

"I can't believe you just asked me to marry you," she said through tears.

"Of course I did, darling Sassy," Ash said, taking his glove off so he could brush away her tears with a warm hand. "I want to build a life with you, wherever we decide it will be. You are my one and only, and you can trust me."

Sassy never dreamed she'd find a man who would break down the walls she'd put up throughout her life, as well as the extra-thick barricade she formed after finding out about her father's deception, and secret family. While it netted her a sister in Kat West, it hardened her willingness to trust—until, that is, she met Ash West.

"What do you say, Sass," Ash smiled that crooked grin that drove her heart and the rest of her crazy. "Will you be my wife?"

CHAPTER 44

The ranch was quiet as midnight approached.

Santa Claus, a big hit with the children, had long ago said his last *Ho Ho Ho* and disappeared out the front door with a wave. After he left, Willow, Sun and Ford played happily with their new toys and talked about how they needed to go to sleep soon, so Santa could deliver the rest of their gifts and fill their stockings.

"He said it, so it's true," Ford said to the girls.

"I wish Grandpa could have been here to see him," Sun said.

"He's old and goes to bed early," Willow wisely said. "But we got lots of pictures. We can show Grandpa in the morning."

While Ridge trudged through the heavy snow to the lower entrance of the ranch, to change into warm flannels and dry slippers, Paislee and Pike whisked all three children into the trundle beds for bedtime stories and sleep.

Rowdy and Daisy had made themselves scarce during Santa's visit.

"We're going to change," Daisy whispered to Kat, then never reappeared.

Kat hadn't seen Ash and Sassy for a while, she noted. Ash took the sleigh and horses back to the barn, and what a night for a ride through the newly fallen snow, she thought, wistfully. Perhaps she'd talk Gunnar into a sleigh ride before the week was through.

"How romantic," she murmured to herself.

Just then, Gunnar came up behind her and wrapped his arms around her. He buried his face in her hair, and kissed the nape of her neck. Kat moaned appreciatively as they stood in the foyer of the house, silent except for soft violins that were dreaming of a white Christmas.

Done, Kat thought, gazing through the transom windows at the snow, starting to fall once again.

"I'm jealous of Ash and Sassy taking a sleigh ride tonight, and not us," Kat pouted playfully. "I think you owe me one."

Gunnar laughed softly in her hair.

"Put it on my tab, woman," he said. "I owe you the world already, one more thing won't matter much."

Kat smiled and pointed to the family photo wall, a hallmark of the massive foyer. "I've got a spot for Rowdy and Daisy's wedding picture, right there," she pointed. "And a place over by Colton and Liu's wedding picture for the twins, Jackson and Jade."

Gunnar shook his head, marveling as they had many times that day, of the new arrivals and how miraculous it all was.

"Twins," Gunnar stated. "I can hardly believe it."

"Me either—I should have guessed," Kat said. "I feel off my game."

"I expect you to guess at diseases, not babies."

"Hmm," Kat said, sounding far away. Gunnar merely held her as they looked at the portrait of Randi Lynn, painted by Pike, and at all the wedding photos. The family had grown and changed so much in the past few years.

"I'm sure going to miss Dad and Casey this winter," Gunnar said.

Kat was secretly glad to hear her husband mention Casey by name as someone he'd come to appreciate and cherish. Never replacing his mother or even trying, Casey had worked hard to become a friend to everyone on the ranch, and she would be missed.

"Willow is going to miss her cousins this winter," Kat said. "And I will too."

"Pike and Paislee are going to leave a void, for sure."

"When they come back in the summer, I'll have a new portrait commissioned with all six of the West grandchildren," Kat said, looking again at the photo wall.

"Sounds nice," Gunnar said, then corrected his wife.

"*Five* grandchildren, don't you mean. Jackson and Jade make five."

Kat was quiet for a moment, and then reached down for Gunnar's hand and moved it to her midsection, placing it firmly on the hard bump of her growing belly.

"Six," she said simply as the clock in the den chimed midnight. "Merry Christmas, Gunnar."

CHAPTER 45

"Consider yourself warned."

Kat had told Daisy and everyone else all about Christmas morning; how the children would be tearing through the ranch house just as soon as the little hand on the clock pointed to the six. There would be no mercy shown; there was no respect for unlocked doors and no time for showers.

"Just throw on your hoodies and meet us in the great room," Kat told the family. "Coffee will be flowing like the water in the gorge, with cinnamon rolls aplenty. First one up puts the sausage on the griddle, and throws the breakfast casseroles in the oven."

"Aye aye, captain," had been the response from Rowdy and others. No stockings could be poured out on the floor until all were present and accounted for, Kat said.

True to her word, mere hours after the last person in the house had fallen asleep, the three children began running from room to room and shouting "Merry Christmas" as they opened doors and rang the jingling hand bells Santa had given them for this very reason. Gunnar cued the happy music as one by one, the Wests arrived, bleary-eyed, in the kitchen.

"Santa came! *Santa came!*" Ford grabbed his uncles and aunts and grandfather one by one and pulled them by the hand to see the stuffed stockings hanging on the fireplace mantle. He held his little arms up for Casey, who lifted him high to get a glimpse at the goodies overflowing from each sock.

"And look under the tree," Willow shouted to whoever was nearby. New wrapped presents bearing Santa's likeness spilled out from below the branches. "He came back, just like he said he would."

Everyone oohed and aahed at the evidence of Santa's visit, while the adults stirred cream into their coffee and made their way into the great room. Already, the aroma of savory breakfast casseroles, stuffed with ham, cheese, potatoes and eggs, filled the air.

"We have a while before the food is ready," Pike said, "so we might as well…"

Ford waited eagerly for his daddy's words.

"…we might as well go back to bed," Pike teased.

The children threw themselves on the floor theatrically and moaned in protest.

"Daddy, we slept all night," Sun said, nearly crying.

"I'm just joking, sweetie. What do you say we hand out everyone's stocking together—want to help me?" Pike kissed his daughter sweetly on her nose, and they got to work.

"This is for you, Grandpa," Sun scolded Ridge, "even though you missed seeing Santa Claus last night, he remembered you."

The family laughed sleepily.

"Well, thank you Sun. I'm always mighty glad to be remembered by Santa Claus."

As the first light of day started to creep over the mountains, the West family warmed themselves by the fire and emptied their Christmas stockings. While the children poured everything out in pile, the adults unpacked one gift after another, exclaiming their surprise and gratitude.

It had become a tradition for everyone in the family to buy trinkets and souvenirs in their travels for just this day. Casey put a pewter brooch from Scotland in each of the girl's stockings; Ash had picked up jars of fruit jam from an orchard in Michigan. Paislee gifted a small book to everyone on walking tours of Denver, hoping to have visitors sooner rather than later. And Ridge cleaned out some of the heirloom jewelry and artifacts he had squirreled away, gifting each West woman a necklace or bracelet from his mother or grandmother, and the men one of his father's sterling silver monogrammed money clips.

"Thanks, Dad," Ash said, "but what the heck is it?"

Ridge took a few large bills from his wallet and demonstrated, then handed the clip back to Ash.

"So Dad, you carry your wallet in the pocket of your pajamas?" Pike's question triggered a string of laughter from the men, reminiscent of their kitchen party from the night before.

"All right, before this gets out of hand, I'm making an executive decision. We have time to open a few presents before breakfast is ready," Kat declared.

Sassy raised her hand shyly.

"Can I give everyone my gifts?" Sassy sat closely to Ash, who had been stroking her arm while wearing a mischievous grin on his face. She got up and searched under the tree until she found a basket full of wrapped presents. While the kids were busy playing with toys from Santa, she stepped around them, and handed the gifts out one by one.

As Gunnar and Pike and Ridge opened the gifts to reveal a single coffee mug from Sassy, Kat and the other women looked around the room with a growing realization.

"Look at the dancing light, Mama," Willow said distractedly.

Indeed, there was a light reflecting around the room with each of Sassy's movements, but the source wasn't immediately apparent to the sleepy women. Until at last, they collectively noticed the sparkling engagement ring on the finger of her left hand.

Kat gasped and stood up with a happy shout at the realization of what the ring meant, followed quickly by the others.

Ridge, who had no idea what all the squealing and shouting was about, held up his mug.

"Merry ChrisMoose," he said jovially to the room.

CHAPTER 46

"Jackson and Jade are doing great," Colton gushed to his family via video chat. "A full day old already, and hungry! I'm sure they get that from me. Good thing mama is a chef."

"Getting any sleep?" Ridge wanted to know.

"A few hours here and there. The hospital provided me with a lumpy recliner chair, but I won't complain."

"When the Wests donate a new birthing wing to the West Gorge Medical Center," Kat assured him, "the dad chairs will be greatly improved."

"Can't we just donate new chairs?" Gunnar asked Kat, who shook her head at him.

"It will be too late for me," Colton joked, "but there may be other West babies in the future, from what I hear." Ash and Rowdy both blushed and Kat stole a glance at Gunnar—she knew he hadn't said a word, as they agreed to keep their baby a secret for a little longer.

"Let me become a husband before you have me being a dad," Ash said, reaching for Sassy's waiting hand.

"You know the Wests don't believe in long engagements," Colton smiled at his little brother through the camera on his phone. "Congratulations, Ash."

Ash grinned from ear to ear.

"Where are the babies?" Paislee pleaded to see the little faces.

"Just coming back from getting their picture taken," Colton said. He leaned over into a rolling bassinet and lifted one little baby who was nestled in a red flannel Christmas stocking. "Here's little Jade, just as pretty as her mama."

The room at the ranch melted into sighs and smiles and sweet laughter at the sight.

"She's a beauty," Ridge said with pride. "Like her mama, but with a touch of daddy."

"And here's my boy, Jackson." Colton set Jade in Liu's arms and picked up a green Christmas stocking, containing the small baby. Jackson opened his eyes and blinked hard at the phone, trying to focus. His sweetheart shaped lips made a sucking sound as he turned his head in pursuit of nourishment.

"Someone's hungry," Colton said. "We'd better go and get these two fed. Can't wait to come home. I have a feeling our big house is going to be a hub of activity real soon."

"For about twenty years," Ridge exclaimed, saying goodbye to his son.

"What a day," Gunnar said, sinking into the sofa he was on and pulling Kat close. He wrapped his arms around her waist and they shared a secret smile. "Thank you so much for my present," he whispered into her ear.

"I told you it was all wrapped up," she whispered back.

As the children played on the floor, Paislee made a sweep of the room with a trash bag and scooped up handfuls of wrapping paper and bows. Casey came in with a tray and removed coffee mugs and breakfast plates, taking them into the kitchen to be washed. Kat could hear somebody taking more of the wedding dinners out of the refrigerator for an early afternoon meal. The big island, she knew, would be overflowing with an endless sampling of cheese logs and crackers, roasted nuts, fresh fruit, cookies, and crunchy vegetables.

"Eat one carrot, then you can have another cookie," she heard Pike say from the kitchen, probably to Sun, who had an insatiable sweet tooth.

Kat smiled at the sights and sounds and aromas of Christmas day. Each year was different and better than the one before. Having Sun and Ford share Christmas morning at the ranch with Willow had been delightful—why hadn't they done that in years past?

Next year, Willow would be joined on Christmas by three babies. She and Gunnar would have to make sure she had a wonderful day, and didn't feel the loss of her other cousins.

She smiled again at the memory of Ridge as Santa the night before. To the adults, he still looked and sounded so much like Ridge, but through the eyes of the children, he truly was Santa Claus. That was so much fun, and she would make sure to thank her father-in-law once again for all the effort he put into pulling the old sleigh out of the barn, and lining it with lights and bells. Casey too. Surely, she helped him as she always does.

"What a day," Kat mumbled to Gunnar as they caught each other's eye. "Thank you for the beautiful bracelet, by the way."

"Hmm, it seems a poor second to your gift," he said. "What else can I give you?"

Kat laughed at a private thought, but then decided to share it.

"I want to see you in that scarf and tam o'shanter hat Ridge and Casey brought you from their trip to Scotland," Kat said with a smile.

Gunnar groaned. "You're killing me, Kat. You don't actually want me to wear it out in public to dinner, in front of other people, do you?"

"No, it's a private showin' I'm wantin', Gunnar O'West," she said in her best brogue.

Gunnar laughed heartily and kissed his wife on the top of her head.

"Merry Christmas, Kat."

CHAPTER 47

"About Chicago," Sassy said to her fiancée. They were curled up on the sofa of the little den, enjoying a private moment away from the chaos of the family celebration. Paislee shooed the children out of the room a time or two, then gently closed the lead glass doors with a wink and a smile.

"Yep, Chicago it is. I'm going to happily move there with you and find a job. Maybe I can be a *barista*—a coffee guy. Or work as a personal trainer at a gym. I'm pretty buff, don't you think?"

Ash flexed his muscles and Sassy touched his arm appreciatively.

They both knew that Ash West had enough money to never work at all, if that's what he chose. Between the West trust fund and generous monetary gifts from Ridge and his own grandmother, he was a very wealthy young man. And while his heart really was at the ranch, and running it with Gunnar and Rowdy, he'd gladly give that up for Sassy.

"I love you for wanting to come to Chicago, but I never got to explain the offer."

Ash frowned. "You don't think I'd let my wife move to Chicago without me…"

"You don't understand," she said. "The accounting firm will

onboard me for a three-month period in Chicago. But then I will be an employee with their remote-work program. I can work from anywhere, Ash. That's why I applied."

Dumbfounded, Ash could hardly believe what he was hearing.

"You mean… you could even work from…" He didn't dare hope, not after making the gut-wrenching decision to leave.

"I can set up my office right here in Wyoming, Ash," Sassy said, "while you run the ranch. I'll need to fly to Chicago once or twice a year for training, but we can handle that, right?"

"Are you saying that you'd consider staying in Wyoming?" Ash still couldn't believe his good fortune.

"I insist that we stay. I've been watching you with your family for several months now, and I am convinced that the best version of Ash West is going to be right here. I see how you draw strength from everyone around you, and how they build you up. I want that for you —and for me, too. At least for now. We may re-negotiate in ten years."

"I can't believe you're making it that easy, Sass."

She smiled to see his happiness.

"Well, I do have a few conditions."

"Name them." Ash meant that.

"We can't live here," she said, indicating the ranch house. "We have to find a home outside of the ranch so my mother can visit us when she wants. Kat deserves that much, and so does my mom."

Ash nodded.

"We can stay in your apartment for now, and try to get on Colton's short list for a new custom-build house. Is that all?"

"I'm going to fly home to Illinois three times a year and I insist that you join me for at least one of those trips."

"Of course. I look forward to getting to know your mom, Sassy. And she'll always be welcome at our home. Is that all?"

Sassy smiled and gazed at the beautiful ring Ash had given her the night before. She thought it was gorgeous in the moonlight, but that was nothing to the details she could now see in the light of day. "Last, I meant what I said about not wanting a wedding—I just want to get married and be married. I want to skip all the attention and hoopla. You okay with that?"

"Wow, you just keep looking better and better, Sassy Tate."

"Sassy *Tate*. I won't have that name for long."

"Not long at all, if I have any say in the matter." Ash turned towards her, then lifted his hand. As he caressed her neck gently, running his hand up into her hair, Sassy closed her eyes and enjoyed the sensation. As her lips parted, they were met by Ash's own. Softly, slowly, he coaxed her towards his open arms. When at last she pulled away, just a bit, she turned her head to breath. She could feel her heart pounding against Ash's own chest.

"When will the courthouse be open again?"

CHAPTER 48

Two days after Christmas, the plows came out in full force and finished clearing the roads in West Gorge. According to the traffic reports, the highways were clear and getting to Denver and Phoenix would be safe.

The Chen family made it to Colton and Liu's house the day before, and now had everything ready for the arrival of the babies. The rooms were warm, the double bassinets were lined with laundered linens, and the food being lovingly cooked by grandmother Chun would help the new mother recover much faster than the hospital offerings.

When Liu first told Colton about the pregnancy, he thought he'd never get a turn holding his own child knowing there were four eager Chen grandparents chomping at the bit—but after a short taste of the demands of twin newborns, he was thankful for the extra hands.

Pike and Paislee were packed and ready for their trip to Denver, where a belated Andrews' Christmas awaited them. After a tearful farewell at the ranch, they would stop at the hospital to meet Jackson and Jade, and say goodbye to Colton and Liu.

"Text when you reach Denver," Kat said.

With tears running down her face, Paislee could only nod.

"Let's hit the road," Pike declared, giving everyone a last hug.

Ridge had tears in his eyes too, Kat could see. Thankfully, he and Casey weren't leaving the same day—one gut-wrenching goodbye a day was enough.

After they could no longer see Pike's car, the family went back inside the ranch.

"It's so quiet without Ford and Sun," Ridge said, wiping away another tear.

"Just wait, Grandpa," Willow said, "Jackson and Jade will be making a lot of noise."

Kat and Gunnar looked at each other with a smile—they would wait and tell their daughter the good news about the baby, soon. It would give Willow something to look forward to. She could help her parents plan and shop for the baby—she'd like that, they knew.

"Maybe we'll take a family trip and buy the little cowboy a few things," Gunnar whispered to Kat, after Willow ran off to her room.

"Can Daddy stop at a few things?" Kat asked with a smile. After revealing the news to her husband about the baby she was carrying, she'd slipped a little note in his stocking, telling him they were having a son.

He was delighted, she could see.

"If anyone wants to take a ride, Ridge and I are going to see his Christmas present—the Craftsman bungalow. Amber is going to meet us there so she can get the house in order before we come home in the spring." Casey stood in the foyer, pulling on her coat and hat.

"How fun to have a house in town," Kat said. "We can have parties on that porch and watch the parades go by."

"Yep," Ridge agreed, putting on his warmest shearling coat and gloves. "My thoughts exactly. Ready Casey girl?"

After they left, Gunnar closed the door again.

"Quieter and quieter," he said.

Rowdy and Daisy had gone home in the morning, and Gunnar told him to take a few days off, but he knew Rowdy would show up at the office. It was that work ethic that took the weight of the ranch off of Gunnar's shoulders—that, and having Ash by his side. They were all glad to hear of the young couple's plans to stay in town.

Kat was delighted to know her little sister would be staying. Where there was once mistrust and pain, there was now love and devotion for each other.

Sassy and Ash were also gone, having an errand to run in town, they said. Probably checking on her apartment and Amber's store, Kat guessed.

Gunnar only shrugged. He was glad to see Ash so relaxed and happy. The troubled lad he'd first met during a hospital quarantine nearly eight years before was now his youngest brother, his ranch partner, and soon he'd be his brother-in-law, once he married Sassy.

Kat turned her eyes from the door and saw Gunnar with unshed tears in his eyes. They walked towards each other and pulled each other close. As his strong arms encircled her, Gunnar kissed the side of her face. She could feel the tears on her skin, and loved the sensation. His heart had become more tender as the years passed.

The proximity to Gunnar and his steady kisses fanned an ember inside of Kat, and she returned his embrace. Soon, they were sharing a slow kiss, growing in its intensity. Tasting him, her breath became more ragged.

"Maybe..." she whispered in his ear as she pulled away from his lips, "maybe you could model that hat and... scarf... for me. In our room."

She could feel Gunnar laugh softly as he kissed her hair and moved his hands to her neck. He knew where to touch her to beckon her.

Her husband was *beckoning* her, and she was helpless to resist.

Finally, everyone had left the house and their busy Christmas was over. Well, almost everyone had left. From the corner of her eye, Kat could see a small movement, and hear mouse-quiet sounds on the inlay floor which caused the lovers to freeze.

"I'm bored," Willow declared with a loud exhale.

CHAPTER 49

"Let's go for a drive," Gunnar said, clapping his hands and startling both Kat and Willow in the foyer. "Daddy needs a little cold air, and I think Mommy does too."

Kat gave him a crooked grin and nodded.

"Yay, a drive," Willow cheered, jumping up and down.

"It's super cold out, so bundle up. I'll come pick you both up by the front door in thirty minutes, okay?"

"Okay Daddy," Willow said happily. She ran down the stairs to the lower level, where all her warm snow suits and boots were waiting.

"Raincheck," Gunnar whispered into Kat's warm ear, then turned to find his own warm things. The sun was shining, but according to the thermometer by the window, it was frigid outside. "Bundle up, little mama."

"I've got my own little furnace working overtime," Kat said, patting her belly. "But yet, I will bundle up. A drive sounds nice."

Maybe, she thought, they'd drive up to Cindy's diner for a burger, or something other than the wedding meals the cheese logs the family had been living on for days. Perhaps they'd stop at the bungalow in town, and see Ridge's Christmas present.

What a wonderful surprise Casey gave him!

There were many surprises this Christmas—the twins, and Pike's family moving to Denver. Ridge and Casey leaving for Phoenix was a surprise too. So was the unexpected change of plans for Daisy and Rowdy's wedding. That turned out to be perfect, though, in her mind. For her own reasons. But she didn't think the couple minded at all. The great room ceremony was perfect, thanks to Ridge. A wedding the family would always remember.

Kat slipped on her long coat, and stepped into fur-lined boots. She found her shearling mittens and hat, and checked herself in the mirror.

"Not too shabby," she smiled at the reflection.

She might be hot once she got into the warm car, but she could easily shuck the layers if needed.

Kat peeked out the window but didn't see any signs of Gunnar or his many cars and trucks. She thought back fondly of the too-big truck he'd picked her up in on their blind date, and how angry she'd been at the choice.

What a neanderthal, she'd said under her breath back then, as she struggled with climbing up and in. She had been wearing a too-tight dress, and her pretty shoe got stuck in the running board. Meanwhile, fielding leers from onlookers in the hospital parking lot, Gunnar took her predicament in his own hands and shoved her in the truck—with his hands fully placed on her rear. Kat had never been angrier in her life.

"I'm a doctor, and you're just a rough-around-the-edges cowboy," she had seethed. That was before she fell head over heels in love. And now look at them. Making out like teenagers in the foyer, and expecting their second child.

She was so blessed by the love of her husband. And sharing their daughter, Willow, had only drawn them closer.

"Mommy, I hear Daddy—but he sounds like Santa Claus," Willow exclaimed as she ran up the stairs, bundled from head to toe.

"Why, he *does* sound like..."

Kat opened the door and saw not a truck, or car, but two horses and the old winter sleigh waiting for them, bells and all. The handsome driver got down and helped Willow up into the seat, then held out his hands for Kat.

"My lady," he said. Kat's delighted laugh could be heard over the snow-covered hills. For Gunnar, the driver of the sleigh, was proudly sporting the wool scarf and matching tam o' shanter hat.

"Shall we?" Her husband kissed her mittened hand and asked, with a twinkle in his eye.

"Oh, we shall," Kat said with a teary smile. "We shall."

CHAPTER 50

Driving to Lander on the last day of the calendar year, Ash and Sassy had to put on their sunglasses to shield their eyes from the bright mid-day sun. The roads were quiet—nearly deserted as they watched the mountain range changing in the distance from tall and jagged, to low and rolling.

Snow capped the peaks and covered the fields in every direction, but the roads were dry and clear, they were glad to see.

Ash hadn't let go of Sassy's hand since they left West Gorge a few hours before. They were quiet in the car, lost in their own thoughts. When at last Sassy spoke, the sound made Ash jump with an abundance of nervous energy.

"Did we just do what I think we did?"

"Um… get a drive-through coffee at the last town?" Ash offered.

"No, not that," Sassy said.

"Oh, you mean pay too much for gas in West Gorge?"

"Not that either," she said. "That other thing."

"Get married at the West Gorge courthouse—*that?*"

Ash squeezed her hand hard and then apologized for his roughness.

"Yes, that. You and I are married, Ash West."

Sassy sighed as if trying to catch her breath after a long mountain run.

"We certainly are, Sassy West, Sassy West, Sassy West. I could say that all day long."

"You'll get lots of practice, I think," she smiled. "Years of practice, in fact."

Ash shook his head in wonder and gazed over at his bride of three hours. She was radiant in her cable-knit sweater from Scotland, and the emerald earrings he'd snuck into her Christmas stocking. Her leg gently bounced with a nervous twitch, until he let go of her hand and placed his hand on her thigh instead, applying a warm, soothing steadiness.

"Breathe," he whispered to her, stealing another glance her way.

Sassy laughed and nodded.

"I've been holding my breath since the first time we kissed, up on the hill. I fell in love with you so quickly, Ash. There were a few times when I couldn't imagine that we would work things out."

"I'm so glad we did. Thank you for marrying me today, and becoming my wife. My heart feels like it's going to beat right out of this fancy flannel shirt you bought me at the Mercantile. After-Christmas sale, right? You bean counters are penny pinchers, I hear."

"It was the good flannel at a good price. Flannel is good. *It's us.* I couldn't ask for a nicer wedding, Ash—thank you for going along with my wishes. I hope you don't feel like you've missed out."

"Never. My only request was a short engagement, and seven days was six days too many. We'll get lots of chances to dress up and dance and celebrate, but today belongs to the two of us alone, the way we wanted it. We'll tell everyone the news when we get back."

"Gunnar didn't mind you taking a few days off?"

"No, he was great. I told him you and I were going to spend some time with Freda and James Timothy in Lander for the new year, which is partly true. We'll have dinner with them in a few days so I'm not made out to be a liar."

"Deal. And I'm happy to be going back to that beautiful bed and breakfast."

"The Lander House," Ash said with pride. "We'll be there soon, only this time…"

"Yes," Sassy said quietly.

They pulled into the parking lot just as the snow started falling. Big flakes landed on Sassy's eyelashes and she smiled with pleasure as they walked hand in hand towards the oversized front door. It didn't take a lot of imagination to picture the lumber baron and his family who once lived in the Victorian mansion.

In the parlor, the silver tree still hugged the corner and lights twinkled in the room, same as the night of Freda's wedding. The night when it had been so hard to go to two separate rooms. The night when Ash declared his love, and they danced and toasted and kissed for hours afterward, at Freda's reception.

The flames in the little fireplace caught Sassy's eye as Ash spoke with the check-in desk.

"Mister and Missus Ash West, welcome and congratulations," the woman enthused. "The honeymoon suite is waiting for you on the third floor and your bags have already been whisked up there by our staff. You'll find crackers, fruit and champagne, and several menus for the restaurants that deliver. You won't want to go out in this snow storm."

"Not for days," Ash said. Sassy could hear the smile in his voice.

As the woman retreated into her back office, Ash and Sassy stood together in the parlor. He reached out shyly and took her hand so gently that she nearly cried at the tenderness.

Yes, she could trust this man. Her husband.

"Off we go," Sassy whispered, giving Ash's hand a squeeze. Just like the night of the wedding, she gently pulled him past the desk, the butler's pantry, and the room marked ICE; only this time, they turned at the wide oak staircase and went up.

When at last they reached the third floor, she turned and said, "this is me."

"This is us," he said, putting the skeleton key in the old door and swinging it wide. Then bending down and putting his arm under her knees, Ash lifted her in his arms and kissed her softly. Both of their lips trembled, until their kiss and their breath found a sweet cadence together. They tasted, and brushed, and caressed until the depth of their kiss had a life of its own. This time, they didn't pull away from each other.

"Let's go check the room for ghosts," Sassy said to her husband as he carried her over the threshold and closed the door firmly behind him.

End

* * *

FIND OUT WHAT KATHY IS WRITING NOW AT KATHYFAWCETT.COM, WHERE you can also read free books, and stay in touch.

OTHER BOOKS BY KATHY FAWCETT

From the meet-cute to the happily ever after, *The West Brothers Romance series* delivers the feel good fun you're looking for in a sweet small town romance.

"I loved this so much I can't wait to read more."

"I wonder what's next for the West clan, and am anxiously awaiting the next book in the series."

The West Brothers Romances:

Her Quarantined Cowboy

Drawing Her Cowboy

Stirring Her Cowboy

Her Sunset Cowboy

Sassy Cowgirl Kisses

A West Ranch Christmas

Plus get *Her Unexpected Cowboy* FREE at KathyFawcett.com

The Lake Michigan Lodge Series

Shoulder Season

Lake Michigan Lodge #1

Kay is finally renovating her lodge and her life. Now who will she share it with? In this funny uplifting tale of renovation, redemption and romance, a rustic old lodge on Lake Michigan isn't the only thing that gets a second chance.

Water Dance

Lake Michigan Lodge #2

Can happy-ever-after survive an invasion of teenage girls? When Kay agrees to hosting her two nieces for the summer, what she doesn't know is where pretty girls are, boys are sure to follow.

And enjoy the romantic prequel *She Sparkles, A Highland Love Story,* FREE at KathyFawcett.com

ABOUT THE AUTHOR

Kathy Fawcett writes sweet romantic comedy and women's fiction that will keep you smiling, crying and turning pages long past your bedtime. Kathy's funny dialogue and heartfelt stories make her a favorite with a growing number of fans. They love the true-to-life situations, happy endings and highly satisfying sequels.

Kathy transports readers to the surf, sand and snow of charming Lake Michigan towns, as well as the windswept mountains of Wyoming.

Home is Michigan, where Kathy worked for years as an advertising writer. She met and married her husband Steve while students at Northern Michigan University, and he introduced her to his home state of Wyoming. Together, they reside near the Great Lakes with their bossy cat Sam, and are surrounded by grown children, grand-children, and towering pine trees. Find out more about Kathy's latest books and projects, get free stories, or email the author at kathy@kathyfawcett.com

www.ingramcontent.com/pod-product-compliance
Lightning Source LLC
LaVergne TN
LVHW010619100826
845148LV00014B/3033